A PERSEPHONE PRINGLE NOVELLA DUO

MURDER AND MICE AND EVERYTHING VICE

AND

TEN HOARDS A-REAPING

PATTI LARSEN

Thanks, Kirstin!

ISBN: 978-1-998948-36-9

MURDER AND MICE AND EVERYTHING VICE

PATTI LARSEN

MURDER AND MICE
AND EVERYTHING VICE

CHAPTER ONE

"And inhale slowly, making sure to relax your shoulders, release your diaphragm. No one's checking to see if your stomach is sticking out, ladies." I grinned at the giggles that comment generated, demonstrating the technique with my own abs rounding forward as I drew in a long, deep breath through my nose. "Now the same in exhale, through your mouth, counting if you need to, all the way to the bottom of your lungs." I finished the exhale and began again, the small class of women seated on meditation pillows in front of me copying with at least temporary focus. While I had no qualms about teaching in such a manner, I found one-on-one sessions with clients much more fulfilling and, for the patient, a sense of accountability that increased probability of regular practice.

"Very nice," I said. "Meditation isn't about emptying your mind. It's about recognizing the thoughts that pass through it, accepting them and letting them go." Before I became a wholistic therapist, leaving my more traditional psychology practice and embracing all methods of therapy, I'd struggled to meditate, thinking I was doing something wrong. Only to discover I was just going about it the wrong way.

"The thoughts are easy, Persephone," one of the ladies said with a grin. "Letting them go, not so much." That got a chuckle from the gathering, including me.

Well, excluding the woman in the back row on the far right who'd been scowling the entire time and, as far as I could tell, refused to participate in any way.

"I thought we were here to learn to be quiet," she sniped, silencing the others while she glared at me like it was my fault the gathered participants weren't taking this seriously. As I was of many minds and techniques when it came to allowing those I worked with to evolve their own practice, I found her attitude irritating. Did the good leader thing and ignored her, though Natasha Lange had proven several times during this first class I guided she didn't play well with others.

"And inhale," I said, wondering again why I'd agreed to this weekend my dear friend and hypnotherapist, Lou Ellen Mallory, decided was a good idea. *Hack Your Habits!* wasn't the kind of event I typically participated in, let alone used as a means to gain patients. In fact, I'd never suffered for lack of those needing my services, so putting myself in this position felt a little like shining a spotlight on ego rather than any sort of successful transition for the women who attended.

Well, as long as I helped at least one person, it was worth it. Right?

The soft music playing in the background was meant to soothe, though I wondered if it was a little intrusive. About as much as the light giggling going on between two of the women who whispered between themselves during the next exhale. Not that I really cared if they took part or not, but I had to admit my inner control freak was already regretting I was here for the rest of today and all of Sunday if this was going to be the result.

"Can't you be quiet?" Natasha wasn't helping, her barked question only making matters worse. She pinned me with an angry stare while the trendy track-suited women snorted their amusement at her temper. "If you can't control the class, you shouldn't be teaching."

So, I'd been in the game a long time, a far cry from my first encounter with those who didn't necessarily want to partake of my offerings, even paying clients who came to see me sometimes only doing so thanks to court orders or their parents or for marriage counseling they didn't think they needed. I was usually pretty quick to refer such reticent patients to other therapists, only keeping the ones that truly wanted to grow and change. I was in a fortunate position financially and professionally and didn't have to tolerate such behavior. Chose not to.

The problem being that this particular setup didn't allow for my selective removal of misbehaving participants. If anything, I felt forced to accommodate and compromise, two of my least favorite words on the planet. Oh, and, "Whatever." If you wanted to rile me up and set me off like nobody's business, trained therapist or not? Shoot me a, "whatever," with any kind of dismissive air and I'd be showing you the door.

My ex-husband's favorite brush-off still rankled and likely always would.

And while I was well aware of my temper, typically able to keep it firmly in check, the circumstances I now found myself in, agreeing to this event despite myself and the fact I now felt resentful for caving in to Lou Ellen, forcing myself to hunker down with twenty-four half-committed (and that was generous) women only here to drink excessively and pretend to better themselves already had me stirred to a bit of a froth.

Natasha's little snarky attack? Lit the fuse on the caldera of my bubbling anger. Not her fault, all mine. I'd agreed to this, chosen to say yes to Lou Ellen and her pleading, to be a good friend despite my reservations. After all, I wasn't against a gin or two myself, nor a laugh here and there when seriousness wasn't working. But I had already moved past patience and into annoyance, so her challenge?

Brought out the worst in me.

"Perhaps if you're not enjoying the class," I said

at my most calm and emotionless—which, if you knew me well, had deep subtext of the rude kind— "you'd prefer to exit and allow the rest of the participants to finish without you."

I knew I'd overstepped the moment the words left my mouth. Honestly, I'd known before I spoke. Natasha might have been new to me as an individual, but she certainly wasn't as a stereotype. I attempted to keep my objectivity in a smothering blanket around my reactionism while her eyes went wide, mouth curving even further downward to the tittering laughter of the gathering that only made things more uncomfortable.

She leaped to her feet, flinging her meditation pillow against the wall, temper tantrum a petulant display that cooled my own anger since it wasn't hard to draw a parallel to the fact I'd acted badly, if in a less physical way. And, as a therapist, I knew better, than rarely was someone's bad behavior aimed at the supposed target but came from deeper issues that had nothing to do with the moment.

So why did I let the moment take over and run away with me?

"Unacceptable!" She tossed her head, round body stuffed into a yoga suit she really needed to have purchased a size up. And before you judge me for body shaming, my continuing fight with my menopausal, fifty-year-old body meant I wasn't a skinny Minnie, by any means, who debated constantly my choices of skinny jeans, cropped blonde hair, and trending clothing my twenty-one-year-old daughter rolled her eyes at. I understood completely what it felt like to be on the other end of the microscope and that our own for ourselves was always worse than what we perceived from those around us. Which meant my judgement of her came, not from what she wore, but my own insecurities. I was aware of all of this, of course I was. Just because I helped others release their anger and sadness didn't mean I was immune or anything.

That's why I felt myself relent a little, almost apologizing then and there. Until she scowled at the other participants, some of whom refused to look her way, others smirking as if this was exactly what they'd hoped for. "I'm going to report you to the organizers." And, with that, Natasha marched out of the room and slammed the door to the parlor behind her.

"Now," I said with a smooth smile that hid the renewal of my temper. "Inhale, slowly through the nose…"

CHAPTER TWO

If Natasha had hung on just fifteen minutes longer, she would have been present to join the clapping that greeted the end of the class, the laughter and chatter of the women who rose from their own cushions, stacking them politely against the wall near the tall windows overlooking the ocean, the towering lighthouse that filled in the bulk of the view behind us a white and red striped echo of the past no longer necessary now that the mainland's automated system warned off ships along the coastline.

I switched off the music playing through the sound pebble I'd brought, keying off my playlist, rising slowly from my crossed-legged position and nodding and smiling to the departing women. While I knew poor Lou Ellen was likely in the midst of fielding a protest from Natasha, I felt lighter despite the conversation I'd have to have with my dear friend once she was done being harangued. Make no mistake, Natasha was a haranguer (that had to be a word) of the most irritating kind and, sadly, was stuck here with us for the duration unless someone called the ferry to return to Bright Point Island and the inn and suites our host converted by building onto the historic lighthouse. Maybe that was part of my problem with the whole event, knowing I was trapped at the venue for two days and three nights with no means of escape unless I wanted to wander into the end of nowhere that was the rocky island. And while I could see my hometown of Wallace, Maine, from the windows, it felt a very long way away indeed, at the tip of Blueberry Bay.

"Ms. Pringle?" One of the women, seemingly in her mid-thirties, who'd struggled to rise using a chair next to her, approached me. Her rounded belly jutted aggressively in its development, enough she had to be in her final trimester. She smiled at me, both hands spread protectively over her baby bump, though I knew from experience with my own pregnancy (was it really twenty-one years ago?) such a touch wasn't conscious but the instinctive caress of impending motherhood.

"Persephone, please," I said, smiling at her waistline. "I know we're not supposed to ask, but I'm assuming there's a baby in there."

She laughed, nodded, dark hair pulled into a ponytail, bright amber eyes alight, that almost-a-mommy glow of pregnancy encouraged by her happy attitude. "Three more weeks," she groaned.

"I'm ready now, but she's not in a hurry so I guess I should be patient." She held out one hand, fingers a little swollen, poor thing, so I was careful when I shook hers. "I'm Daphne Hampton. Thank you for the class. The breathing is a big help and I hear meditation can really calm things down when I'm waiting for labor to speed up."

"You'll do just fine," I said.

"I'm not the most patient person," she said. Glanced over her shoulder at the doorway and the mostly departed participants. Eye rolled and let out a breathless laugh. "Not like you. I'd have kicked her out ages ago." She paused then while I hesitated over what to say since I was here as a facilitator and not a gossip, saving my griping for Lou Ellen. "I think I should warn you, though," she said. "I know Natasha. She's a bit of an internet critic celebrity, in case you didn't know. She makes it a habit to ruin people if they make her mad." She bit her lower lip, shrugged as though making a decision, her tone falling flat, happiness gone when she went on. "She's a monster. Loves making trouble." Daphne glanced over her shoulder one more time. "If I'd known she was going to be here, I wouldn't have come."

Sounded like Lou Ellen had her hands full and I'd made her job harder. Not that I felt badly for the way I dealt with Natasha, not in the least, despite that moment of hesitation and empathy I'd almost fallen into. While I could still feel compassion for the woman, if this was her bread and butter, she'd get nothing of the sort further from me. People like her couldn't be fixed because they were happy being broken. However, I certainly owed my friend an apology if I made trouble for her. Lou Ellen's hypnotherapy business was only beginning and I may have nipped any chance she had of success in the bud with my temper.

"Thank you for the warning," I said, a gentle hand on Daphne's shoulder. "If you or the baby need anything, please don't hesitate to ask."

We emerged together into the hall outside the parlor room where I'd held my first session, most of the participants already in the dining room, the loud sound of talking carrying from the doorway where coffee and snacks awaited us. Which meant nothing stood between us and the sight of the very woman we'd been discussing having a hissing and visibly nasty conversation with another guest.

I gestured for Daphne to precede me into the dining room, jaw setting as I squared off to confront the troublemaker, but I was too late, Natasha storming off past the woman she'd been berating. I could have hunted down the former, but it seemed the latter's distress was more immediate and my compassion kicked in over the surge of my pique.

"I'm Persephone," I said, offering a kind smile to the small, older woman, her lined face tight with anxiety, brown eyes shining with unshed tears. She sniffled a little, looked down as though embarrassed to be seen that way, hands shaking as she fished a tissue out of the pocket of her baggy blue sweater, dabbing her nose and eyes with it before offering me a weak smile of her own.

"Fern Baker," she said, voice trembling. "Nice to

meet you, Persephone. I wanted to take your meditation session, but it was full this morning."

"I have another tomorrow," I said. "I'd love for you to join me."

She bobbed a nod, composure returning, tissue vanishing back into her pocket, hands running down the front of her t-shirt to the waistband of her old-school gray sweatpants. "That's very kind of you," she said. "I'd love to."

"Did you get a snack?" I guided her toward the dining room without asking questions about her interaction with our resident trouble maker, wanting to talk to Lou Ellen first. She was the host, after all, and I realized I'd failed to ask some rather important questions. Like, how did she want me to deal with someone who clearly took pleasure in making other people miserable? While trapped with said person on an island with no way off until this was all over?

I really hadn't thought it through. Not that I cared if Natasha gave me a hard time, but I couldn't see even my kind-hearted and (occasionally) flaky (don't tell her I said that) friend tolerating that kind of behavior for long.

By the time I had Fern situated with a cup of tea and a cinnamon roll, I had decided if Lou Ellen wasn't going to take Natasha in hand, I'd do it personally. If Daphne was right and the woman's intent was to cause issues down the road, I was in a better position to take it than my friend, since I was fully established with faithful clients and a reputation with the local hospital and legal teams while Lou Ellen's practice might not endure a social media onslaught intended to hurt her reputation.

Was it wrong I kind of hoped Natasha would come for me so I could squash her arrogant butt? Yes, but I wasn't judging myself for it. Some people just needed a life lesson now and then and I was a therapist, after all.

I paused at the doorway to the hall, stepping out from the group as they socialized, planning ahead to my next session in fifteen minutes, wondering if I should adjust my offerings to something less weighty. If they could barely keep their attention on simple meditation techniques, would they get anything out of more advanced opportunities to deal with old trauma?

Only one way to find out.

Movement out of the corner of my eye had me squinting, the inn's ginger tabby cat slinking by. I had nothing against her kind, to the contrary. I hadn't been able to have a kitty since meeting my ex-husband, twenty-four years of no pets thanks to his allergies always a bone of contention between us. Not that Special Agent in Charge Trent Garret was the pet kind anyway, FBI superhero persona not exactly the emotionally squishy type. No, my glare had nothing to do with the cat herself, per se.

Instead, it was the memory of finding a dead mouse in my bathroom this morning that gave me a wee bit of the willies and raised my concern. Then again, if the poor perished rodent was left there by said Ms. Kitty, she was just doing her job and I shouldn't be judging her for it.

She vanished around the bottom of the bannister

and galloped up the steps, the sound of her footfalls fading.

"Ms. Pringle?" I turned, smile appearing instantly, the young woman offering her hand to me triggering my instinctual reaction to be welcoming and open.

"Persephone," I said, reminding myself to tell everyone to call me that from now on, but in a group setting so I didn't have to keep repeating myself.

"Dr. Shauna Raine," she said, dark blonde hair in a tight braid, the faintly rough and calloused feel of her palm surprising me, as did her broad shoulders and inches of height over mine. "I'm in your next session. You're teaching us tapping? I've heard such good things. Can it help with a fear of heights?"

And just like that my hesitation over offering my favorite tools perished.

Even as the sound of a woman screaming smothered the warm feelings and spun me around, to race down the hall toward the source of the sound with my heart in my throat.

CHAPTER THREE

In case you missed it, I was more of a run toward a problem kind of girl than away from it, though you'd think after fifty years on the planet I'd have learned a bit more in the way of self-preservation. Maybe it was my penchant for poking my nose into other people's troubles (invited or otherwise), or my drive to help, to heal, that dictated what some called courage and others audacity. Regardless, I was the first to reach the doorway to the downstairs bathroom, to whip open the entry and step across the threshold, expecting to find a murder going on at the very least.

Instead, I exhaled in a gust of exasperation at the sight of none other than Natasha Lange, still shrieking like a banshee, pressed up against the sink counter, pointing at the small, brown bundle of fur, immobile on the gray tile floor.

A mouse. She found a dead mouse. Seriously?

Someone pushed past me, our host, Helen Stewart, in a clear state of frazzled disarray mirrored in her wavy brown hair, the rumpled appearance of her logoed golf shirt, the dusting of what looked like flour on her black shoes and the cuff of her uniform pants. I noted that frazzled seemed to be her normal since she'd been a bit of a nervous wreck since we'd arrived, barely hiding it under a veneer of almost hysterical welcome.

"I'm so sorry, I'll take care of it immediately, please, it's all right." Helen lunged for the little creature, scooping it into her bare hands and spinning to exit the room, hurrying past me while I fixed Natasha with a look that I tried to moderate into understanding but knew barely hit flat displeasure.

For her part, she spluttered, face bright red thanks to her overreaction, chubby hands fluttering in front of her chest, sneakers squeaking on the floor as she spun toward me.

"Disgusting!" I'd only seen a few people spitting mad until this point in my career, two of them high on something, the other caught in the act of a crime. Natasha had it down to a science, droplets flying from her lips, caught in the faint sunlight coming in from the narrow windows near the tall ceiling. "A rodent. In the washroom." She was clearly looking for some kind of backup, and while I'd endured my own dead mousie in my own private space just an hour ago, I'd managed to refrain from losing my freaking mind, so sympathy wasn't forthcoming.

"Are you all right?" Hey, I managed to be nice. Well, at least I asked. Not sure if nice was part of it, but I tried.

Natasha didn't bother responding, forcing her way past me though I dodged her before she could do any shoving, realizing she then had to push by a gathering as it appeared the bulk of the attendees had come to stand outside the door to see what all the fuss was about.

Lou Ellen slipped into the bathroom beside me, her silver curls piled loosely on top of her head, the flowing multi-colored kaftan she wore over her wide-legged, pale blue pants skimming the tops of her bare feet, a small silver ring on her right middle toe sparkling. As did the multitude of silver rings on her long, narrow fingers, wrists jangling with bangles as she took my hand and led me deeper into the space, smiling and waving at everyone who still lingered.

"Thank you, it's fine," she said. "Go back to your snacks. Next session starts shortly."

With the excitement over, the participants retreated, door swinging shut. The moment it did, Lou Ellen's tight smile collapsed into an anxious expression, hands wringing, making her rows of shining bracelets ring. "Tell me I didn't make a huge mistake and things are going well?"

Whoops. Should I inform her then and there or lie to her and let her have a brief break from what looked like a growing set of nerves.

While I adored Lou Ellen, had known her since high school and always got along with her, she had a terrible habit of wanting to only see the bright side of things and digging herself in deeper than she should, forcing other people to rescue her more often than not. Okay, I wasn't being entirely fair, but if she couldn't handle a few bumps, she shouldn't have dove head-first into this idea.

I told her about Natasha's fit in my class and added Daphne's warning, to which Lou Ellen groaned softly.

"I know," she said. "I'd hoped if I made a good impression, she might promote me and the retreat."

"Not looking promising," I said. "If I hadn't pissed her off, the dead mouse likely means a one-star rating for the inn, at the very least." Now I did feel bad, hugging her impulsively, before letting her go, gripping her upper arms in my hands, smiling despite the sour note we'd just shared. "It'll be fine," I said. "Everyone else seems to be having a great time. You can't let one person ruin it for the rest."

Lou Ellen's expression firmed, chin rising, smiling back at me. "You're right, Seph," she said, hugging me back. "This is exactly why I asked you to join me for the first event. I knew I could count on you to keep my head on straight." She fluffed her curls with both hands, the wild locks of her soft and halo-like mass of silver untouched by color ever. We were a bit of a contrast, her a hippy, new age, earth goddess and me with my dyed blonde pixie and plethora of tattoos. We might have been the same age, but fifty looked far different on her than it did me.

What was it they said about opposites and

friendship?

"I'll deal with it," Lou Ellen said. "You didn't do anything wrong."

I knew that already. Sighed, shrugged. "Come on," I said, grabbing her hand, dragging her to the door. "Let's go find her so I can apologize before I change my mind and choke on it."

The beaming smile my friend shot me was worth it. I guess. Mostly.

We'd see.

Wouldn't you know, the only way Natasha would accept said making of amends was in front of everyone. "I want a public apology," she sniffed in my general direction when Lou Ellen and I confronted her outside the dining room a minute later. "For her rudeness." She didn't even look at me, focused completely on Lou Ellen. I knew why. It was obvious she knew she could bully my friend, took the low road and did so while I ground my teeth and hung in there for the hypnotherapist's sake. "I felt unwelcome in her session. I thought this was supposed to be an inclusive retreat, not a chance for a clear egomaniac to belittle your participants."

She.

Egom—

Choke.

She'd get an *I'm sorry* over my dead—

"Of course, no problem." Lou Ellen might as well have cut my throat. I met her eyes with my temper hitting the back of my throat in a blow that came so close to me laughing out loud before telling the nasty piece of work where she could fling herself off the side of the island. Only to stop, absorb my friend's desperate need for this to work out, cutting my proverbial legs out from under me and putting me in a terrible position.

Whether Lou Ellen knew it or not, asking me to follow through decimated any kind of respect or standing I might have held, undermining not only me and my professional credibility, but my ability to connect with and teach the women who'd come here for my expertise.

I almost said no. Inhaled, exhaled, followed my own practice of just a short time ago. Turned to the smirking Natasha with her narrowed piggy eyes and smug expression and nodded. Before stalking into the dining room with her and Lou Ellen trailing after me.

"If I could have your attention." I backed off my aggression when I saw it register on some faces, the startled looks I got from a few of the participants reminding me it wasn't Natasha who would undercut me. It was me. My choices, the way I handled the next few minutes. And I planned to come out ahead, you better believe it. "Thank you, first of all, for putting your faith in me, in Lou Ellen." I gestured at my friend who waved and smiled, though she looked nervous. She should. She knew me very well and had to be shaking in her bangles over what I might do and say. "This weekend is meant as an evolution for you, a chance for you to confront things you'd rather no longer plagued you, to relieve yourself and your life of issues that hold you back." They all nodded, smiled. "In doing so, we all confront things that bring out emotions, sometimes overwhelming, sometimes uncomfortable." I gestured at Natasha who was now glaring. She must have known where I was going with my "apology" and I had to fight the smile of triumph that rose in response to her discontent at my rebellion. Oh, I planned to give her what she asked for. Just not the way she wanted it.

Groveling was not in my lexicon.

"If, at any time, I raise such discomfort in you, I deeply and sincerely apologize." I nodded my head to Natasha. "But please know, those moments of distress are necessary, signposts from your own personal Universe that you've struck on an issue ready to rise to the surface and exit you and your life." I wasn't talking bunk. I honestly believed every word. Though, in Natasha's case, it would have taken a lot more than one issue clearing, but I digress. "So, please, accept my regret at your discomfort but celebrate that feeling and step into it." I held out my hand to her while she looked around, everyone beaming, hope nearly palpable in the room, the other women gathered there caught up in the moment, even Lou Ellen clasping her hands under her chin, tears in her eyes. "Natasha, I'm so sorry your discomfort led us to conflict. Can I help you repair the hurt and free you forever?"

I wasn't sure what to expect, honestly. Half of me hoped and suspected she'd accept, just let it go. But the rest of me was pretty sure someone like her simply couldn't back down. When her scrunched expression turned to defiance, I had my answer.

"This is ridiculous," she snarled before spinning

and stalking out of the room while everyone stared and watched her go.

Leaving me standing in the middle of the space, hand still extended. No way was I letting this opportunity pass. I had a chance to really reach them, to make a difference, even if that meant a performance was part of the job.

"Let's all hold Natasha's hurt in our hearts," I said, the murmurs of the others in agreement. "And be kind to one another and ourselves, knowing such conflict can be defeated if we face it head on."

Lou Ellen applauded, the rest of the gathering following suit, while I fought off that feeling of being a fraud that sometimes arose when I made a spectacle of myself.

I exited then, heading for the front door, breezing past Lou Ellen before she could stop me. "I just need some air." Pushed out onto the stairs down to the stone pathway, turning immediately to the right and away from the walk onto the grass, heading for the side of the building and around the corner so I could be alone for two freaking minutes.

Covered my butt or not, I realized I'd come here for the wrong reasons with a terrible attitude and part of this was my fault. I was letting Lou Ellen down, far more than I would have if I'd said no. So it was either suck up my own issues and do what I promised or be a jerk and a whiner and mirror Natasha.

Yeah, not going to happen. If anything, her whole hissy fit nastiness was the perfect reflection of my own inner whiner and, while grateful for the poke to pay attention, I at least was willing to do something about it even if she wasn't.

I would smile and be sweet and tolerant and kind from now on.

That decision made, I paused at the base of the lighthouse, looking down over the cliff with my heart in my throat, old remnants of my fear of heights mingling with my curiosity, a narrow stairway carved from the rock leading down to the bare skim of beach and a small dock, with what looked like a rowboat tied up to it. The ferry dropped us on the other side of the island, where it sloped down to the water in a more accessible grade. The thrill of standing there with one hand on the centuries-old stone and daring the edge made me smile.

As did the utter calm, the almost glassy ocean barely undulating, despite the soft waves that reached the shore. I could almost believe in anything standing there, even my own ability to do as I promised and not make Lou Ellen regret inviting me. Or myself for saying yes.

I turned to head back in, lungs filled with salt air, spotting someone up ahead near the small shed tucked into the shadow of the towering lighthouse. Helen was just emerging from it, the innkeeper's jerking, nervous walk hurriedly carrying her back toward the main building.

Apparently, I wasn't the only person who needed some fresh Atlantic Ocean air. The sight of Daphne circling the shed, Fern and Shauna, the unlikely pair with their heads down and chatting away like old friends, appearing from the other direction. The intrusion had me pausing, not wanting to have to talk to anyone just yet. I let the three women finish their curious investigation of the surroundings and then carry on before I finally set out for the front door again and my next session.

Everything was going to be just fine.

Keep telling yourself that, Pringle. The Universe was listening.

CHAPTER FOUR

My request was apparently accepted, because the rest of my sessions unfolded without a hitch, lunch a delicious chowder with homemade biscuits I drooled over before allowing myself one and chiding my hips and tummy for welcoming the carbs with open arms.

Even the afternoon flew by, many of my participants excited and a few having breakthroughs during session, so by the time we ended to get ready for dinner, I was feeling much more optimistic. It helped Natasha had apparently retreated to her room to sulk, and though that fact wasn't going to help Lou Ellen in the long run it certainly made my life easier for the time being.

The only real hiccup? The two dead mice I found on my bedspread when I arrived back in my room. I grimaced at the offering, wondering why the cat would leave them for me. Did she like me? I'd heard that, how felines would deliver what they thought of as gifts to those they appreciated. Or, wait, did she think I was starving and needed the food more than she did? Whatever her reasoning, I planned to have a chat with Helen about finding out how the cat was getting into my room in the first place while I carefully wrapped both tiny carcasses in toilet paper and deposited them in the trash under another quickly bundled strip.

Not that I stood there and had a moment for them or anything. A mouse funeral seemed like a bit much. I did catch myself looking around more carefully and jumped once or twice when I imagined something running across the floor while I changed and touched up my makeup before descending to the downstairs in rather more of a hurry than I'd gone up.

I wasn't squeamish about it, but I did expect a certain level of rodent-free accommodation. Surely that wasn't too much to ask for?

With my shudders firmly in hand, I headed for the back hall and the kitchen, finding Helen in a solid state of what looked like panic as she single-handedly wrangled dinner while I gaped at her.

"You're alone?" I hurried toward her, taking the masher from her hand as she labored over a giant pot of potatoes, the poor woman huffing off to the counter where she grabbed an icing bag and proceeded to pipe a large tray of cupcakes with a bit more reckless speed than was probably good for the confections. Then again, as she flew through them, I realized her deft and steady hand meant more than enough practice she could handle it.

"My cook got sick," she grunted, "and the two girls I hired as maids didn't show up." No wonder she seemed frazzled. Helen paused to wipe at her forehead with the back of one hand, her brown curls threaded through with enough iron gray she'd earned them, blue eyes tight and apron covered in flour and other foodstuffs. "It's fine. I can handle it. Please, don't worry."

I finished mashing, setting the utensil aside, hoping she wouldn't realize I was terrible in the kitchen before I could convince her to let me assist. "Just tell me what to do," I said. "I'm here for you."

The relief on her face made me want to hug her.

She had me stirring gravy next, while she finished the cupcakes. I hesitated to ask her about the mouse issue, not wanting to add to her troubles, and let it go for now. There would be time to bring it up after dinner, when she wasn't so overworked. The last thing I needed was for her to accidentally poison us because I'd upset her.

It was clear to me we needed to recruit more aid. "I'll be right back." I stepped out into the hall, planning to wrangle Lou Ellen to assist before Helen could protest, only to spot Daphne outside the bathroom door, Natasha in her face, the pair in a clear argument though the hissing nature of it made it impossible to know what the conflict was about. Well, the pregnant woman had told me she knew Natasha, so it was possible this confrontation had to do with whatever past they brought with them.

More surprising was the sight of Fern, a small movement giving her away, where she had tucked herself just inside a doorway with it almost closed on her, though she was clearly eavesdropping. When she spotted me watching, the small woman flinched and slipped out again, heading away from the arguing pair, leaving me to shake my head.

Hey, I'd been known to listen in on a conversation or two in my day. For all I knew, Fern wanted to go to the bathroom but had no desire to again have to deal with Natasha. Whatever her reason for running off, it was hers and hers alone.

The fight broke up, Natasha entering the washroom, Daphne heading for the dining room, their departure a bit of a relief since I already had an issue to handle and wrangling them would interfere with dinner being served. I waved to Lou Ellen who emerged from the dining room door, noting Shauna entering the front door at the same moment, both of them coming toward me, though it was clear Shauna realized her mistake right after my friend headed my way.

"Helen needs us in the kitchen," I said to Lou Ellen, smiling at Shauna. Fern peeked out, came our way as well, joined us as I tried to figure out how to send the two participants off without letting them know we were kind of in a pickle.

"It's dinner," I said at last. "Helen's staff didn't show."

"I used to serve in college," Shauna said, super casual, no judgment.

"I was a line cook at a diner," Fern said, voice

27

very low and almost apologetic.

"Perfect." I grabbed my friend, pushing her through the door and into the kitchen, motioning the other two to follow. "I'm sure Lou Ellen will be happy to give you a refund for the assistance."

And that's how I saved dinner.

You're welcome.

CHAPTER FIVE

The only glitch in the evening's offering was the encounter with (you guessed it) a few more unwelcome furry guests, one that squeaked at me when I opened the pantry door and hoofed it out of sight faster than I could inhale in surprise, and two more that apparently the cat had already taken care of but again left behind after creating said carnage.

I was beginning to think the ginger huntress a bit of a savage with a penchant for serial killing, no snacking to be seen. Maybe the thrill of terrifying the poor little rodents into heart failure—not one had a mark on them—gave her the joy she needed to make her life worthwhile. Though I'd heard cats were rather ferocious and cunning murderers without any sort of compassion for their prey, I was starting to wonder where this particular kitty was finding all of her new playmates.

That thought had me alarmed enough I vowed to ask questions of Helen once dinner was successfully wrapped up.

Once the bulk of the creating and serving was complete, I was able to slip into my seat at the large dining room table, helping myself to the roast chicken and a small dollop of potatoes I'd so faithfully mashed, a thick slice of homemade bread and real churned butter making me groan in appreciation. While Helen might have been on her own, she'd been determined to deliver, and had she. What could she accomplish with a full staff, I wondered? Unless the sea air and hard work (mental and physical) had altered my appetite, this was honestly the most delicious food I'd had in ages.

I noted that while she did join us for the meal, Natasha didn't speak to a soul except to snap at seat mates to pass things she couldn't reach herself, almost knocking over someone's wine glass when they didn't move fast enough for her liking. And though she cleaned her plate and took seconds, when Helen came to the door with a weary and nervous smile to ask how everything was, our resident complainer was the first to speak up.

"The chicken was cold," Natasha said, "and I found lumps in my potatoes." Everyone stared at her, mouths open, me included, why the ironic continuation of her filling her own gaping maw did nothing to silence her whining. "And we ran out of butter at this end of the table."

Helen rushed instantly forward to offer the partial dish from a quickly responsive guest, Natasha taking it without thanks while I glared and barely kept from commenting. The only thing that silenced me was the pinched, unhappy expression on Lou Ellen's face and the fact that I was positive if I focused hard enough I could do something awful and permanent to Natasha through sheer will alone and never be blamed for it because my awesome mental abilities were untraceable.

Yeah, I was living in a fantasy world. Do you really blame me?

"That was delicious, Helen," my friend said, everyone else aside from the still eating Natasha murmuring their agreement. "Thank you so much."

Helen bobbed an awkward little curtsy before heading back to the hall and the kitchen, I imagined. I thought about getting up, going to help her clean up, and decided to give myself a minute for my food to digest while talk fired up around the room again.

"—mouse in my closet," someone said to my right. Whoops, had to deal with that issue.

"—gave me a headache, but I think it was my fault when I forced that pose." Another complaint, likely due to one of Lou Ellen's self-hypnosis yoga sessions. I never did get into that form of exercise, nor hypnosis itself, aside from using suggestion to help clients get into the moment, the only place they were able to heal anything.

"—storm front," another voice said to my left. "Freak weather off the coast—"

"—sister would have loved this," that was good to hear. "I'll bring her next—"

"Seph." I hadn't noticed Lou Ellen stand and

circle around behind me, too busy eavesdropping on conversation snippets. I looked up, smiled, noted her tension and sighed as I joined her, exiting and heading for the kitchen. While not my job, we couldn't have the owner of the inn pass out on us because she had to do everything herself.

Except, when we were about ten feet from the dining room, Lou Ellen stopped and turned to face me, hesitant and more than a little anxious.

"I'm not sure I want to do the demonstration tonight." She'd been looking forward to it, planned a live hypnotherapy session for one or more of the guests, not quite a show but close enough.

I could guess why she hesitated. "You're worried Natasha will want to participate." That could end one of two ways. In total and utter disaster when the horrible woman proclaimed Lou Ellen's method was a waste of time and in total and utter disaster when… well. You get the idea.

The problem was, she'd printed it in the itinerary and I knew many of the guests were looking forward to it. "It'll be fine," I said, knowing that word was about as inadequate as any, didn't wince, but close enough. "Just pick someone else. I'll run defense, okay?"

She flashed a smile that held only nervousness. "Okay. If you think so."

Oh boy. Don't put this on me, woman. Not my retreat, not my monkeys.

Though, as the ladies assembled in the larger sitting room at the front of the main building, all twenty-four in attendance and even Helen coming to stand at the doorway to watch, I realized it kind of was my responsibility for all. And had every intention of shutting Natasha down at the first sign of trouble.

As for Lou Ellen, she seemed to have settled by the time everyone was ready for the session to begin, folding chairs assembled in the middle of the room, regular furniture pushed back out of the way. Her smile lit her face, as genuine as ever and her kind and compassionate heart shining in her eyes.

"I'd love to guide one or more of you through the evolutionary process of transformational hypnotherapy." Smiles and whispers followed, a few hands going up, everyone eager for the experience.

All my plans to protect Lou Ellen ended in a crash and burn when, instead of waiting for her turn, Natasha instead stood up and marched uninvited to the front of the room, plonking herself (oh yes, so graceful) into the seat beside my friend and crossing her arms over her substantial chest.

Well, craptastic.

"It's not all about you, you know." I was surprised Daphne spoke up, her lovely face creased in anger. "Though I wouldn't expect someone like you to put other people's needs ahead of yours."

Natasha scowled at her. "You chose to get pregnant," she snapped, "so you deal with the morning sickness. I was born with this condition." Her haughty tone screamed denial and unwillingness to actually do anything to commit to what it took to change. She was the epitome of an impossible client and I didn't envy Lou Ellen one bit.

My friend, rather than deny Natasha, instead reached out and gently freed her hand, holding it between her own. The normally resistant woman seemed startled by Lou Ellen's gentleness and didn't fight, Natasha sitting forward a little when the hypnotherapist nodded to her.

"In order to assist you," she said, "I'll need to know what condition it is you'd like to address tonight."

Natasha wriggled in her seat, the glance she shot at the gathering clear indication of her sudden discomfort. "I have a food addiction," she said, sharp enough she had to have expected some kind of pushback, even ridicule.

Self-fulfilling prophecies often came from familiar places. Daphne's barking laugh was followed by some hissing disapproval from others, but she ignored them. "You don't say?" She seemed to enjoy the chance to humiliate Natasha, as though turning tables had been her hope all along. "Never met a cupcake you didn't like, right, Tash?"

I almost (almost, so close, like, *this close*) felt sorry for Natasha in that moment. No one deserved to be treated that way, especially in a room of grown women. This wasn't high school. Then again, she'd been the one to bring it up, obviously knew the reaction she'd get from Daphne since they were already acquainted (and maybe more than that). I held off interfering while Lou Ellen ignored the heckler and focused on Natasha.

"Addictions of that type are so hard to deal with on your own. I'm happy to help if I can." Natasha's nose wrinkled, mouth still turned downward, but she didn't protest Lou Ellen's words. "Shall we begin?"

I knew from the get-go my friend would fail. Whatever willingness her patient might have felt initially, whether Natasha intended for this to work for her or not (cynic here knew not), there was no way Lou Ellen was getting through to the grim, antagonistic and walled-off woman who glared at the hypnotherapist the entire time, not even attempting to follow instructions.

I had to hand it to Lou Ellen, though. She didn't quit on Natasha, not once, trying everything she could to soothe the savage beast. But when it was obvious the woman wasn't even going to close her eyes, after about ten minutes of encouragement, Lou Ellen finally let Natasha's hand go and sat back with a sad smile.

"Hypnotherapy is a powerful tool," she said, "but only if you'll let it be."

Helen had just walked through the door, a tray of cupcakes in her hands. I spotted Daphne, saw her evil grin, moved to cut her off but was too late. The pregnant woman had a confection in hand and was hustling faster than someone in her late stage should have been able, just in time with Lou Ellen's words to shove the sweet treat in Natasha's face.

"Hear that?" Daphne laughed, not a pleasant sound. "It's your fault after all."

Natasha stood abruptly, surging to her feet, grabbing the cupcake from Daphne. Her glare challenged everyone in the room. "Just like a hack to blame me for her fraud not working." She made no mention of Daphne or her interruption, pouring all the guilt on Lou Ellen. "Just as I expected. This whole weekend is a sham and a waste of time and I'm going to make sure my followers not only avoid it in future but ensure neither of you," how nice of her to include me in the attack, "ever practice your flimflam ever again."

Natasha stormed off out of the room, past Helen who ducked out of her way, the rest of the participants watching her go before Daphne did a slow-clap at her exit.

"If you want even a taste," she drawled, "you'd better get it now, ladies, because Tash will be in the pantry at 2AM eating everything you leave behind."

That was about enough of that.

CHAPTER SIX

I topped up Lou Ellen's gin with another ounce, adding some ice and a splash of cranberry before pouring myself my second. She sipped silently, staring out into the still and star-filled evening as the pair of us sat on the narrow balcony just outside my room, enjoying the warmth of the late June sea air.

She tucked the sweater she'd borrowed from me around her narrow shoulders, the sound of her bangles missing now that she'd taken them off, leaving them behind in her room when she came to see me for a bit of comfort.

"This was a terrible idea," she said.

"It'll all work out," I said. Saluted her. She clinked back but without feeling. "She's one crazy person, Lou. Seriously."

"You know I don't like that term," she frowned at me.

That made me laugh. "I'm the degreed psychologist. I'm the one who isn't supposed to use words like that. The thing is, it's just a word, Louie. We can't heal what we're afraid of." I sipped gin, so glad I left the academic part of my job behind for the exploration of what really healed people. Not talk. Action. While many of my compatriots wouldn't agree, I found much more success in allowing my patients—clients, Seph—to use tools to uncover their buried hurts, not talk endlessly and just relive it and the trauma all over again.

Lou Ellen emptied her glass in two big swallows, set it aside before I could refill it again. "You're right," she said. "I will not let one woman and her clear intent to ruin this weekend ruin this weekend." She stood, hugged me awkwardly from that position, and left with a soft good night.

I took my time finishing my gin, wondering at how calm the evening felt, before heading to the bathroom to rinse both glasses in the sink and stopped at the threshold when I turned on the light.

Sighed at the dead mouse on the floor and performed what I hoped was my last funeral before going to bed.

I really had to talk to Helen.

A crashing roar of thunder woke me, paired with the thudding swing of the window I'd left ajar as a gust of wind slammed it against its hinges. It took me about ten seconds to get over the bleary realization, to slip out of bed, now hissing my displeasure in the sudden chill, to catch the wavering window bobbing from the airflow pressure and to close and latch it firmly against the sudden shift in weather.

What had been a deliciously calm evening turned to what looked like the beginning of a storm front, lightning flickering close enough for discomfort while the building rocked from another gust. With the now ten-degree temperature drop making me shiver, I quickly donned a robe and slippers, even as another giant flash of lightning, this one illuminating the entire sky for a moment, crashed somewhere in the vicinity of our power source.

How did I know? Because the moment it hit, the entire distant town of Wallace went dark and so did all ambient light from downstairs. Amazing how much even a little bit of brightness can be ignored, the clock at the bedside table now black, the sounds of distress from other rooms loud as doors slammed, voices calling out, asking what happened, as the building shuddered under yet another buffering from the Atlantic's firm breath.

I hurried out into the hallway, doing my best to calm and reassure on my way to the stairs, followed by the swarm of now wide-awake women who'd joined us for the retreat. The thunder had woken everyone, it appeared, enough illumination from following lightning strikes helping me find my way down the steps to the main floor.

Someone had a flashlight, Helen's face appearing behind it, already on her way to the front door. "I'll start the generator," she said. "I'll be right back."

I almost went with her as wind whipped the entry from her hands, but stayed put instead, hating the thought of going out in the now frenzied gusts and rumbling thunder that prowled over the island and much of the coast, if the now black skies devoid of stars or a moon meant what I thought they did.

"There's an underwater cable," Lou Ellen said, appearing suddenly at my side, wrapped in the sweater she'd borrowed from me earlier. "I checked before I booked."

"Lights out on the mainland," I said, keeping my voice down. "Helen said something about a generator."

"Ladies," Lou Ellen turned to address the gathered women who, despite the startling events, seemed cheerful enough. "I'm so sorry about the interruption of your beauty sleep. Not that any of you need it." That generated laughter if not electricity. "Our host is restoring power now, but I'm sure if you want to go back to bed everything will be right as rain by morning."

Helen returned that exact moment, shivering, her flashlight casting eerie shadows down the main hall, and giving her eyes a sunken expression. "I'm so sorry," she said, sounding near to tears. "The generator is… it's not working." I hugged her around the shoulders, the poor dear. She'd been through a lot since we'd arrived, dealing with everything on her own. Helen smiled weakly up at me, though I could see the gratitude in her eyes. "We'll have to wait until power is restored on the mainland."

"Who's up for a late-night hangout?" I was surprised to hear that from Daphne, the pregnant woman grinning. "I haven't stayed up all night since I was a teenager. Might be fun. We could get candles?" She spoke that last as a question to Helen who nodded. "Roast marshmallows." That was greeted with more laughter and nods of agreement. "Snacks?"

"I'll put some things together," Helen said.

"I'm telling the first ghost story." Daphne led the ladies into the large sitting room, Lou Ellen going with them, while I let Helen go with a reassuring smile.

"It'll be fine," I said. "There was nothing you could do."

Helen hesitated then tossed her hands, brilliance flickering as her flashlight protested. "There's candles in the pantry," she said.

I'd seen them earlier, nodded immediately, faint golden glows appearing in the sitting room as some of the decorative ones in that space were lit. "I'll get them," I said. "And snacks." Nodded to Shauna who appeared at the door, eyebrows raised.

"Need help?" She joined me, the broad-shouldered woman smiling at Helen. "My dad's a mechanic. Want me to look at the genny?"

"Perfect," I said, even as Helen seemed to want to protest. "I'll take care of this. You two go see about power." And left them, heading for the kitchen in the dark because I'd lost my mind.

Lightning offered enough guidance, hitting with

41

regular frequency, my arrival in the kitchen much faster and without stubbed toes I'd been half-expecting. The pantry I had to wait for, hurrying when a flash landed over the water, making it to the door with a breathless little laugh. This was actually kind of fun, an adventure. No wonder Daphne responded the way she did. She was going to make a great mom.

Which had me thinking about my daughter and the fact I should have brought Calliope, though my worry wart child who was too much her father for her own good likely would have been too anxious to enjoy herself.

All thoughts of my kid and her disappointing lean toward Trent's way of being died (if you'll forgive the terminology) when the next hit of lightning showed me the interior of the pantry. And more than I bargained for.

This time, instead of a perished mouse, or a live one, even, I had the misfortune to, in the creepy flash of bright, white light through the kitchen window reminiscent of a horror movie, come face-to-face with the staring and lifeless face of Natasha Lange.

Mouth open. Filled with what looked like icing.

She'd eaten her last cupcake.

CHAPTER SEVEN

My first instinct was to call Trent in a desperate panic. Second? To internally smack myself for even considering I needed my ex-husband to ride in and rescue me. The whole point of divorce was learning to stand on my own two feet, right? While I realized that didn't always apply in all cases, it did give me pause long enough to keep me from freaking out at the sight of Natasha's dead body.

I'd seen a few before, of course I had. Losing my dad hadn't been the happiest memory, and although this was a far cry from beeping machines in palliative care while he slowly slipped away thanks to cancer, at least I had some experience with the empty nothingness of death. And, a healthy dose of curiosity that, after the initial fright only compounded by the circumstances of finding her this way while in the midst of a power outage caused by a massive freak thunderstorm (cue the creepy Hollywood music that meant the heroine really needed to turn around because the killer was right behind her), I was able to rein in my fright. With my wits firmly around me, I retrieved the box of candles I'd come for, along with a lighter next to them in the following flicker of light before retreating and firmly closing the door behind me.

Not that out of sight meant out of mind in this case, but I'd take it for now.

First things first, of course. I headed back to the main hall and to the entry, Helen and Shauna returning when I flagged down Lou Ellen with my cargo.

"Something's been at the wiring," Shauna said, shrugging. "Unfortunate, but it's beyond my ability to fix."

Helen's face had that pinched and unhappy look that told me she knew exactly why the generator wasn't functioning and so did I. The plethora of mice I'd encountered (and who knew how many the others had as well) had to suggest some kind of infestation the inn's owner clearly didn't want exposed. If that had been the worst of our problems, I might have brought it up. Instead, there were more pressing matters—one in particular—so I let the rodent problem fall to the wayside in favor of the dead woman in the pantry.

"I take it you have an emergency radio?" Helen nodded immediately, that tightly controlled anxiety releasing somewhat when she realized I wasn't going to push the subject. Just wait until she found out why. Oy. "Will it work without electricity?"

"It has a self-winding mechanism," Helen said. "Creates its own power. It should be enough to reach the mainland if we need it to."

I glanced at Lou Ellen, hesitating, only because Shauna was there and I didn't want to share what I had to say with a participant. Chose a different line of questioning instead.

"Do we know if anyone is a doctor?" I winced inwardly, because even that query implied things that had the trio all staring a moment. Wait, hadn't Shauna introduced herself as Dr. Shauna Raine?

Confirmed it by speaking up. "I'm a vet." Shauna shrugged again, her broad shoulders lifting and falling under her light jacket. "Will I do? Is someone sick?"

"Not exactly." Okay, out with it, Persephone Pringle. "Follow me, all of you, and keep your voices down."

Helen's flashlight didn't improve the view all that much, though at least none of the three lost their crap on me. The inn's owner did pale out quite a bit, mouth hanging open, while Lou Ellen hugged my sweater around herself, tears rising in her eyes, shining in the reflected illumination.

Shauna, for her part, gulped and then stepped forward after a brief glance at me. I nodded, encouraged her to investigate, holding still and waiting for her to do a cursory examination. A box of decorating gloves caught my attention, perched next to me on a shelf, so I retrieved a pair, handing them to Shauna who took them without a word, crouching next to where Natasha had fallen against the far wall, the partially empty plastic container of tonight's remaining cupcakes in her lap. Daphne's little speech about just this circumstance had me wondering, even as Shauna turned to look up at us, grim, head shaking.

"I can't tell if it was natural causes or not," she said. "It could be a heart attack."

Without some kind of analysis it would be difficult to find the truth. Except, as Shauna gently opened Natasha's mouth, I noted the cupcake frosting seemed to be dyed red instead of the blue Helen used and realized it wasn't buttercream but a trace of blood.

"That can't be normal," I said.

Shauna sat back on her haunches, hands dangling between her knees. "There's some evidence of internal hemorrhaging," she said, pointing out spots in the woman's milking over eyes and a rim of red in her nostrils. "Was she on any kind of heart meds? Blood thinners?"

"We can check her room," I said.

"If it was a heart attack," Helen blurted, "why does it matter?"

I exchanged a look with the vet who was the one who spoke up.

"Because it might have been murder," Shauna said in a heavy voice. "This kind of bleeding suggests she took a high dose of bromadiolone or some other anticoagulant." She glanced at Helen then back at me. "Like the kind they use in rat poison."

And now we were all staring at the innkeeper

because, yeah.

"Helen," I said as carefully and gently as possible while she backed away, shaking her head, free hand over her mouth, eyes bulging, "I've noticed you have a mouse problem."

She sobbed once, still denying it with her short, dark hair threaded in silver catching light as she shook it and shook it over and over again. A soft moan escaped her, Lou Ellen reaching out to hug her while I freed Helen of the flashlight and changed the subject.

"How about ways off the island?" I had to wait for the innkeeper to inhale, to catch her breath, staring at me as though she didn't hear a word I'd said, lost in the fear she displayed so clearly I had to repeat myself. "Helen, are we stuck here until the ferry comes or is there an emergency access to the mainland?"

She swallowed thickly, cleared her throat, leaning into Lou Ellen as her gaze returned in a horrified stare to Natasha's dead body. "A rowboat," she managed at last while my mind clicked, memory reminding me I'd seen the very thing at the bottom of the cliff, the small dock at the base of the treacherous stairs down to the beach. "But the waves, the storm." Helen returned her attention to me, still in shock. "It's too dangerous."

Okay then. "That means if this was murder," I said, "whoever killed Natasha Lange can't get away."

Not one of us spoke for a long moment. Because I was sure they were thinking the same thing I was. While the killer couldn't leave, that meant we couldn't either. And if this wasn't a targeted murder but some crazy serial poisoner?

I needed to call the mainland immediately. I handed off the flashlight to Shauna. "We need to keep this quiet," I said, just as Fern Baker joined us, her entry unnoticed until the moment she started to scream.

Then turned tail and ran from the kitchen.

So much for quiet.

CHAPTER EIGHT

The resulting pandemonium wasn't unexpected, however, I was surprised at how quickly the group settled down once Lou Ellen interrupted Fern's panicked reveal.

"I'm asking all of you to stay calm," my friend said in her kind and confident voice, "while we do our best to deal with this tragedy."

"Tragedy my butt," Daphne snorted, looking around at the others, some of whom didn't seem all that broken up by Natasha's death, either, though there were enough guiltily horrified looks the rest might not have lost any sleep over the woman's passing but weren't about to express it so blatantly. "How did she die? Death by cupcake?" Her little laugh finally perished itself as Lou Ellen's face fell. "No, really?" That garnered a bark of hysterical giggles from the pregnant woman. "I was just kidding, but did she choke on one or something?"

"We're about to contact the mainland," I said, stepping in while whispered speculation raced around the room. "I'd like to ask everyone to remain here, together, while we figure out the power issue and talk to the sheriff." At least, I hoped I could get through to Cherise King. My friend and Wallace's lead in law enforcement would know what to do, her years as a homicide detective before immigrating to our town to take over as sheriff exactly the kind of experience I needed access to right now. Had me wishing the statuesque woman with her deep voice and gorgeously glowing dark skin and eyes, corkscrew curls in a tight crop of no-nonsense, had attended this weekend. Thing was, I knew she was likely dealing with her own troubles back in Wallace if the power was out to the whole town. But talking to her would reassure me we'd be seeing help arrive sooner rather than later.

"At least we know who did it." Had Fern meant to blurt that out loud? All eyes shifted to the small, older woman who huddled on the corner of a sofa, the regular furniture returned to create a more cozy space, putting the bulk of the women in a face-to-face where they sat in a circle around the room. The tiny woman trembled on the little bit of cushion she occupied, staring at Daphne in horror and open fear.

The pregnant woman didn't realize who Fern was accusing for a long moment, looking around until she finally caught on as many of the participants refused to meet her eyes. Daphne's next laugh crackled with derision, dying off when she took in the reactions of the others.

"You can't be serious," she spluttered.

"I heard you two fighting," Fern said. "You said she was the reason you got divorced."

Well now, that was rather interesting. Except Daphne waved off that particular tidbit with an eye roll and a grimace, hands then falling to her swollen belly.

"My idiot ex-husband might have decided to have an affair," she said, "but it's good riddance, I say. She can have him. I won the lottery this time around, ladies." She flashed the large diamond ring set on her left hand, the impressive jewelry tight on her thickened fingers but, I had to admit, substantial. "She did me a favor. Besides, do you think I'd risk my daughter or a life with her when all I've wanted is to get pregnant over someone like Natasha?"

Okay, I believed her, if only because I was a mom and there was honestly nothing I wouldn't do to protect Calliope. But kill someone out of revenge and put my kid at risk? That made no sense.

Fern seemed to be second-guessing as well while I held up both hands for attention.

"If we could refrain from accusing each other of murder," I said at my most sarcastic, a few giggles following, "since we're not even sure it wasn't natural causes," except I was pretty sure, but they didn't need to know that, "how about we let the police decide while the rest of us do our best to weather this and support one another." I hadn't meant the pun, but it seemed to help, another round of nervous laughter following it while I grimaced.

"Thank you. We'll keep you up to date but, for now, let's make the most of this terrible situation."

"If anyone would like to talk or needs grief counselling, we're here for you," Lou Ellen added, reminding me I'd kind of just walked all over her position as event leader, but she'd forgive me.

Why wasn't I surprised no one made a move to take her up on that offer? Whatever kind of impression Natasha Lange left behind, it clearly didn't generate any sort of compassion from this group.

At least we didn't have a weeping mess to deal with along with everything else.

I headed back to the kitchen, Shauna following, knowing I had to do something about the body and, with her help and a pair of decorating gloves on my own hands, grunted and manhandled the corpse into the walk-in fridge so it wouldn't start decomposing. Who knew how long we'd have to wait for help to arrive? Helen anxiously shifted the food we were meant to eat (I'd be avoiding meals that didn't come out of a prepackaged box for the duration) while we spread the white tablecloth she provided over Natasha's corpse, tucking in the edges to keep her contained, the box of cupcakes closed and slipped into a garbage bag.

"Shauna," I said, "have you noticed dead mice on the property?" As a vet, she must have jumped to the same conclusion I had.

There was that grim expression again. "You think someone's been poisoning them."

I nodded, both of our gazes turning to Helen as

the frazzled innkeeper sat at the center island after our terrible task was done.

"You think she killed Natasha?" Shauna leaned in a little, her voice low.

"I have no idea," I said. "But you mentioned rat poison as a possible cause of death, and if the dearly departed rodents I've been stumbling on have died from unnatural causes, someone could have found and used that same substance on the cupcakes."

Shauna swallowed hard. "I had one earlier," she said. Shook her head immediately. "We'd all be showing symptoms by now."

"Which means if someone did poison the cupcakes, they did so after we all had ours." I thought about it a moment. "How long would it take to kill her?"

"Depends on how much she ingested," Shauna said. "Looked like there were four or five wrappers, yes?" I agreed with that guess. "Not long. Especially if she had a preexisting heart condition."

"Wouldn't she notice the taste?" I swallowed myself, stomach tight.

Shauna shook her head. "It's made to taste good," she said. "That's the problem, why so many children and small pets end up accidentally dosed. But it's not as effective in mice, so I'm surprised Helen's using it. They typically have to eat it more than once, unlike rats."

"And the inn's cat?" Poor thing. Now I worried about her.

"If she's not eating them," the vet said, "she's a smart cookie. She must know they aren't safe.

Hopefully she's getting enough food she's only hunting."

My anger finally surfaced. "I thought this kind of poison was banned in Wallace." Didn't a little girl die last year? I couldn't remember the details.

Shauna nodded, glancing at Helen who stared into nothing, rocking herself a little. I really needed to check on the woman because if she'd settled into shock, she would need to have someone sit with her.

"Council passed a law eight months ago," the vet said. "Some local farmers are still using it. Our warm winter last year meant a boom in rodent population. It could be Helen's having an outbreak and decided to take matters into her own hands."

I'd be having a chat with the woman about that, make no mistake. But first, I had a sheriff to talk to.

CHAPTER NINE

With the evidence preserved as best as I was able, I made one more stop before attempting to call Cherise. Helen instantly gave me access to Natasha's room, the pill bottles in her bathroom revealing she was taking something called warfarin. The vet took the bottle from me, nodded.

"Blood thinner," she said. So Shauna had been right. The poison acted fast thanks to the woman's pre-existing heart condition.

Next, I sent the vet back to the others with my thanks while Helen led me to the radio, tucked into her small office in the back of the building. The small radio with its plastic hand crank fired up easily enough, though I wasn't sure how effective it would be in reaching the mainland, especially under the circumstances. But, within moments of me attempting contact, a nervous, "This is Bright Point

Island, come in?" I heard a squawk of response.

"This is Sheriff Cherise King from the Wallace Sheriff's Department," my friend said, a wash of relief at the sound of her voice making me sag. "Is that you, Persephone? Over."

"It is," I said. "Power's out on the island, generator non-functional and..." I paused, not sure what to say. CB radios weren't exactly protected from outside listening, after all. Anyone on this channel could hear what I had to say.

"You have to say over when you're done, Seph," Cherise said. "Over."

"Sorry, I have a delicate situation and I'm trying to be cautious. I need assistance as soon as possible. Over." She wasn't going to let me leave it at that, though, was she? And if Cherise decided it was fine to discuss over an open channel...

"Understood," she said. "We'll do our best, but the storm snuck up on all of us. Is there need of ambulatory or medical service? Over."

"Not anymore," I muttered before keying the handset. "Just get here as fast as you can," I said. "Over."

Cherise's intuition had to be tingling. "You okay, Seph? Over."

"I will be when you get here," I said. "Over."

"I'll be in touch ASAP," she said. "Be safe." Paused. "Over."

"Bright Point Island out," I said, setting aside the handset with a sigh. Looked up at Helen. "We need to have a conversation about the rat poison you have hidden somewhere on the premises, and don't try to deny it."

Helen burst into tears, sitting next to me in the spare office chair. "I'm so sorry," she wailed. "There were so many mice and the exterminators couldn't come for a week and you were all booked in. I had to do *something*." She calmed a little, face wracked with anguish. "My brother, Jake, has a farm on the mainland. He showed me how to use the stuff. I'm really careful, I swear! I keep it in the shed, away from the main building. No one should even have known it was there."

The shed. I'd seen any number of participants out there earlier. Wait, yesterday morning, I guess, since we were well into the wee hours of Sunday by now.

"Please, I had nothing to do with that woman's death, I swear it." Helen now wrung her hands in her lap, distress making her knees bounce as her lower lip trembled. "I just needed to protect my business."

While I could understand the sentiment, the practice not so much. "Do you keep the shed locked, Helen?"

Her mute expression told me the answer before she shook her head, still crying. Which meant anyone could have wandered in there and taken some of the poison. The killer must have realized the dead mice on the property meant someone was killing them. Or had brought their own poison with them and Helen's rodent problem was just a coincidence. I had to admit, however, Daphne's comment about Natasha eating late-night cupcakes just felt too coincidental to be ignored. Either the pregnant woman had killed her or she'd given the murderer the perfect suggestion to follow through with a plan perhaps they hadn't even considered until she handed them the means and opportunity.

I just had to figure out motive. Though, since it seemed everyone here couldn't care less the woman was dead, uncovering her killer might prove impossible.

Wait, what was I doing? I wasn't Cherise or my ex-husband. No sheriff or FBI special agent. I was a wholistic therapist, for goodness sakes. It was not my job to figure out who killed Natasha Lange, just to preserve what evidence I could and keep everyone happy until help could arrive.

Unless. If this was just the opening salvo of some insane serial killer? Could I sit by and wait to see if someone else was going to die? Maybe the murderer took out Natasha first on purpose, knowing no one would cry over her loss?

No. I had to get a grip. The storm, the poison, the means of her death… all amounted to the sort of synchronistic opportunism that a vengeful person without a real plan might impulsively act on. The likelihood anyone else was at risk plummeted to about zero.

Why then was I still intent on finding out who did it?

Just nosy, I guess.

When I finally headed back to the main room, Helen in tow, it was to a fight just breaking out, shouting rising in volume as I hurried to the door, finding Daphne holding a tablet up, pointing at Fern, everyone yelling over everyone else while Lou Ellen tried to calm them down by adding her own voice to the mix.

I'd learned early in life how to whistle through my fingers, one of those silly skills that came up as useful on occasion, case in point. The shrill sound had them all falling silent in a flash, everyone turning toward me, Daphne speaking up first before my friend could tell me what was going on.

"No wonder she accused me," the pregnant woman said. "She's trying to hide her own involvement." I crossed to Daphne, looked down at the image on her tablet she pressed into my hands, then up at Fern who huddled, in visible misery, in the place I'd left her, now shaking violently, starting as though terrified someone might attack her. "This is proof," Daphne said, "that Fern Baker was one of Natasha's targets." Indeed it was, the blog post from what looked like the dead woman's website featuring none other than the shaking Fern. "She ruined your diner," Daphne finished, with enough spite and vitriol I wondered about her own state of mental health, "and you killed her for revenge."

CHAPTER TEN

"Daphne," I interrupted her triumphant moment, everyone staring in shock at the accusation, "there's no internet. How do you have access to Natasha's website?"

She had the good grace to blush, look down. "I'm not online," she said. "I make copies of all of Natasha's victim posts." Her chin went up, challenging the others to say a word. "Not because I wanted to hurt her. Someone needs to do something about her, that's all." She stopped, eyes widening. "Not *murder*," she said. "Just… it's not fair, what she does to people." Now completely flustered, the pregnant woman took the tablet back with a rather abrupt tug, pressing it to her chest like she was protecting it just as she had her baby. "She was a terrible person who did terrible things to nice people."

"It's true." Fern's teeth chattered as she rocked in place, her hands clutching an afghan around her. She started as thunder rolled, the lightning lighting the room so brightly for a moment I blinked stars after. "I wasn't just a line cook. I owned my own place. And Natasha ruined me, demanded free food all the time. I finally said no and she wrote that post. Said my kitchen had cockroaches, that I had issues with the health department." Fern wept, shuddering when more thunder rattled the windows. "I had the inspector visit one day she was there, that was all. Didn't matter. Natasha's hate won and her followers ruined everything."

I'd heard of such things happening, the anonymity of online communities turning into mobs that smothered businesses and individuals so quickly and thoroughly there was no way to recover. If Natasha did so to Fern, I had nothing but sympathy for her.

But Helen's inhaled, "ah-ha!" and quick exodus had us all waiting a long moment for her return, clutching what looked like her guest book. She handed it to me while Lou Ellen came to join me, the innkeeper pointing at the registry with a shaking finger.

"Ms. Lange didn't pay for her own ticket," she said. "She made a huge deal out of telling me so when she arrived, that someone sent her one. I assumed it was Lou Ellen or you, Persephone. But, if that's true, why did Fern buy two tickets and come alone?"

I was with the entire room when we turned to the

trembling woman. This time, when the sound that followed the flash shook the building, Fern leaped to her feet and ran past me, dropping the afghan as she fled the room.

Of course, I spun and pursued her. Though where her guilty conscience thought it could take her I wasn't sure.

This time, when lightning hit, the bolt struck so close I feared it might have hit the lighthouse, the entire island seeming to tremble as the loudest clap of thunder I'd ever heard had me crying out in surprise and fear.

I wasn't the only one, Fern collapsing on the floor just inside the main door, screaming. By the time I reached her, she'd fallen silent and it wasn't hard to realize why. With her eyes rolled back in her head and body falling limp, it was clear Fern Baker's ability to handle stress had ended in unconsciousness.

"Here, let me." Shauna knelt next to me, lifting the small woman effortlessly into her arms, carrying her next door to the sitting room where I'd held my sessions. She gently laid Fern out on one of the window seats, Lou Ellen appearing with the afghan Fern shed in her flight. I tucked the woman in with a pillow under her head, just as her eyes fluttered and she came back to us.

The moment more thunder rolled.

Fern sat up abruptly, hugging me, sobbing while I rubbed her back and realized it wasn't guilt that had her so worked up.

"How long have you had a phobia of thunder

and lightning, Fern?" I didn't push her away, but she yielded anyway, lying back, panting, hands clutching at her chest in a way I feared for her heart, though her panic subsided a little as I softly held her wrists.

"My brother was hit with lightning when we were kids," she whispered. "He died. I've been scared ever since. I can usually shut it out, but it's so loud and close." She sobbed then, tugging free of my grip to cover her face in her hands. "Are we going to die?"

"No, Fern," I said as gently as I could. "It's going to be all right." I nodded to Lou Ellen. "In fact, we're going to do everything we can to make sure you never have to be afraid again."

She nodded beneath her hands before letting them drop, eyes meeting mine. "I sent her the ticket," she said, voice trembling. "I didn't kill her, though. I just wanted to watch her." I'd been witness to that behavior, so I nodded. "To find out her secrets."

"To do to her what she did to you." I understood, even if I couldn't condone.

Fern wept again, Lou Ellen taking my place. I turned to find Shauna had already left, headed back to the main room and the others.

"I thought I asked you to refrain from accusing one another?" No laughter this time, just guilty stares. "I know you're scared. But I spoke to the sheriff. She knows we need her and she'll be here just as soon as the storm clears." She hadn't said as much, but they seemed to take the news to heart, so I hoped Cherise wouldn't keep us waiting long.

I debated having everyone go back to their

63

rooms, noted they seemed content to stay together, joined Daphne on the divan she'd claimed, her weary face finally showing she'd changed her mind about the state of affairs.

"How's the baby?" She might have overreacted to Fern's accusation and turned it on the other woman, but I could understand that need to defend her unborn child and herself.

"Active." Daphne wrinkled her nose at me. "I'm sorry," she gushed then. "I shouldn't have accused Fern like that. We're all worked up."

"Understandable," I said, pointing at the tablet. "Do you mind if I take a look at the posts?"

She handed it to me, tucking herself under the throw she pulled from the back of the daybed. "She was truly a despicable person," Daphne said. "And so are her followers. They took pleasure in ruining businesses and lives. Sometimes I wonder if it's even safe to bring a life into the world. Why are people so cruel?"

"I wish I knew," I said, skimming the posts she'd saved on her tablet, shaking my head. "We have this need to belong, to be part of something bigger than we are. And there's so much fear, all based on fighting against things. As individuals, I'm sure the majority of Natasha's followers are good people. But we can get swept up in a wave of emotion and momentum sometimes without realizing we're hurting others. The first time we see what we've done, we can think we did the right thing. But it gets out of hand so fast until it's cruelty for the sake of belonging." I paused at one of the entries, frowned.

Realized in that moment the killer had been under my nose all along.

Looked up. Caught her eyes. Knew she knew.

As Shauna Raine rose to her feet and, without appearing to hurry, strode out the door.

CHAPTER ELEVEN

I was just fast enough to spot her heading for the kitchen, disappearing through the door, and had to run to catch up. I was so intent on catching her, I skidded to a stop and ran through into the dark room without considering the fact she was pretty jacked, not to mention taller than me and about fifteen years younger.

Except she didn't pause to fight, was fleeing out the back door into the storm, when I finally realized how stupid I was being.

She couldn't go anywhere, after all. There was no way off the—

I started running again, didn't call out for help, didn't think to let anyone know where I was going. All I could think about was what Helen told us while Shauna examined Natasha's body. About the cliff and the stairs and the rowboat at the bottom. And while the innkeeper may not have thought the small craft ocean worthy in such a storm, it was clear to me Shauna Raine didn't agree with her.

At least I knew exactly where she was going.

I almost tripped over the silly cat who lunged for the door when I opened it, ducking out into the rain for her own reasons. Not my problem since I had a killer to catch and she was obviously capable of taking care of herself.

It was easier to see outside, ambient light from the storm above as sheet lightning carried across the clouds much more frequent than the long bolts that dove for the water. The rain had tapered off, at least, even the wind seeming to retreat somewhat, though it still felt like a bit of a battle slipping and sliding over the grass toward the edge and the lighthouse as I circled the tall, white structure as fast as I dared.

Stopping when I reached the far side at the sight of Shauna, hovering at the lip of the steep staircase, hesitating. Her own vertigo issues like the ones I'd felt earlier? The participants all came with their own habits, phobias and vices they wanted tackled. And didn't Shauna say prior to attending my tapping class she struggled with heights? She hadn't brought it up in the session, but I was sure she mentioned it.

"It's a long way down." I had to shout to be heard as thunder followed right on the heels of a fresh flash of lightning, wiping water from my eyes, wind stronger on this side of the lighthouse, rain slapping my cheeks. Shauna turned toward me, more of nature's brilliance illuminating the terror on her face.

"Don't come any closer!" She held out both hands toward me, panic and desperation at war. "Just stay back!"

"You won't make it, Shauna," I said. "Even if you manage to get to the beach in this wind and rain, the boat will sink out there." I pointed to the giant whitecaps heading for Wallace. "You'll capsize, drown. Come back inside. Let's talk about it."

"I didn't come here to kill her, you know." Shauna's voice ached with hurt despite the volume, none of her angst getting lost. "I had no idea she was going to be here. I came to clear the things holding me back."

"She was one of them," I said. "Because of your father."

She flinched, hands falling to her sides slowly as if she'd forgotten why she had them raised. "I worried Daphne might make the connection, might have that blog post on her tablet. When I saw you talking with her, scanning them, I knew you'd figure it out."

"Your father's mechanic shop was shut down," I said. "The photo she used, you're in it." She nodded. "Natasha accused him of overcharging and ripping off clients."

"My father," Shauna shouted suddenly, fury in her tall, wide-shouldered body, rain plastering some of her dark blonde hair to her cheek as she practically spit into the wind, "was the most honest, good and kind man I ever knew."

"He's still alive, Shauna," I said.

"After her relentless attack drove him to a

stroke," she shot back. "Dad was the only person who ever believed in me, helped me get into vet school, supported me while I studied. He was a good person, and she ruined him. Ruined everything." Shauna wiped rain from her face, turned to look down the stairs, her terror gone. "I had to put him in a care home. He's barely sixty-five and he doesn't even know who I am." She took a sliding step toward the edge. While confronting phobias under duress wasn't my suggested method of eliminating fear, sometimes all it took was a deeper one to shift the first out of the way.

I had to keep her talking. And though triggering her issue with heights again by reminding her of what she feared was probably the better choice, I couldn't in good conscience use her phobia against her. "You knew Helen was poisoning the mice," I said.

Shauna turned back to me. There was that characteristic shrug of hers. "I'm a vet," she said. "Of course I knew. It was easy to find, too. I figured she'd keep it somewhere out of people's view and the shed was the obvious choice. I wasn't going to do anything. And then Natasha was awful to you and she kept being more and more awful to everyone. I overheard her say she was going to create three separate blogs, one for this place, one for Lou Ellen and one for you." She shook her head then. "I couldn't let her ruin anyone else. I'd let it go on too long."

"You realized Daphne's suggestion was the answer," I said.

Shauna's hands rose and fell. "It was so simple. I

just… dosed the icing. Helen left them out on the pantry shelf, in that container. Took about a minute to mix it into the buttercream."

"Shauna," I said. "What if someone else had eaten one? Did you think of that?"

She shuddered, face contorting in the light of a bolt hitting offshore. "I snuck downstairs after everyone went to bed," she said. "I waited to see if she'd take the bait. Almost delivered them to her, but Daphne was right. Five minutes after I was done, Natasha showed up and that was that." Her face contorted, begging me to understand. "I wasn't going to let anyone else get hurt."

A murderer with a conscience who'd justified it to herself.

"I'm not sorry she's dead," Shauna said then, shoulders squaring, body swaying with the wind. She'd made some decision in her own mind, I could see it in her stance, hear the decisiveness in her voice even over the wind. "I thought I could get away with it, get back to the mainland before anyone figured it out. The storm came up, but it happened after she went in the kitchen. I didn't realize until the power went out I was in trouble." She stopped talking a moment, fixing me with a grim expression. "You're right, I won't make it to shore in that." She pointed over the cliff. "If I even make it to the bottom alive. But I have to try."

I lunged for her, a stupid, stupid idea, knowing even if I did catch her she'd fight me and we'd both probably go over the edge.

But I wasn't the only one out here with Shauna,

as it turned out. I spotted the ginger streak a half second before the inn's cat, a tiny dark mouse racing ahead, skimmed around the edge of the lighthouse and between Shauna and the first step. While she may have had control of her terror for the moment, I heard the vet scream as, startled by the interruption, she slipped on the grass, lower body sliding out from under her, flipping over on her stomach even as she went over the edge.

Panicked eyes locked on mine.

I don't remember how I got there, to the lip of the cliff. Would later have zero recollection of moving the distance between me and her. All I could recall in hindsight was the touch of her hands as I caught both of hers before she could slip away completely, grunting when I landed on my belly on the ground, pulling with all my might to keep her from falling.

Shauna's feet scrabbled on the steps, pushing her upward, until she lay, panting and sobbing, beside me, rain and wind buffeting us both, lightning followed by thunder a chorus for her weeping while I gently held her and tried not to let my compassion get the better of me.

CHAPTER TWELVE

Sheriff Cherise King arched a perfectly shaped eyebrow at me, grinning with those shining, white teeth flashing against her gorgeous dark skin, her tall body in full uniform, black and khaki suiting her. She'd tucked her mirrored aviators into her short hair, shaking her head at me as her two deputies escorted the cuffed and compliant Shauna Raine to the ferry dock.

"I'll talk to Helen," Cherise said, her shoulder receiver muttering with voices she turned down as she spoke. "But she's looking at a pretty steep fine for the poison."

As she should, though I did feel for her. "Thanks for getting here so quickly." The storm cleared off about an hour after I saved Shauna, the vet coming back inside with me and quietly waiting for authorities to arrive to my surprise. Maybe the near-death experience had been enough for her. Or, perhaps, it had been what I said when we reached the kitchen again.

"Your father wouldn't want you to kill for him," I said. "Or die, either."

Whatever her reason for giving up the fight, she wasn't my problem anymore. Not that the compassion that tried to win a few hours ago wasn't still giving me angst. It would for a while, I think, because while Shauna was a murderer, I wasn't above admitting in her position? I wouldn't promise I'd hold back, either.

A chattering line of women walked past us, heading for the ferry and the mainland.

"Power's still out," Cherise said, "but it won't be long before it's restored. You coming home?"

I nodded, waving to Fern Baker who waved back, though she didn't stop to talk, while Lou Ellen joined us.

"I did my best to help with her fear," my friend said. "I think it worked. She made it through the rest of the storm and seemed okay."

I hugged her. "You did an amazing thing for Fern." Thought about it. "Just, next time you decide to have one of these things? Don't ask me. I'm busy."

Lou Ellen laughed sadly, Cherise joining in.

"Sounds like you might be ready for a change of career anyway," my sheriff friend said, winking at Lou Ellen. "Now that you're divorced from that FBI guy, maybe your real life purpose is showing up."

Not that Cherise and Trent didn't get along and

were, in fact, friends. He was the reason we had her as our sheriff, a case they worked together in Chicago years ago sparking a friendship that culminated in Wallace being lucky enough to have her. So her teasing made me grin instead of groan.

"Yeah, no thanks," I said, arm around Lou Ellen. "That's the only dead by unnatural causes I'd like to encounter for the rest of my life. Not to mention murderer."

"Amen to that," Lou Ellen said.

Cherise took her leave as two EMTs emerged from the main building with a body bag on a stretcher, my friend sighing at my side.

"I'm so sorry, Seph," Lou Ellen said, melancholy weighing her voice down. "This was a terrible idea."

"No," I said, leading her toward the ferry and our waiting bags, time to go and put all this behind us. "You keep doing you. Meanwhile, I think I need a retreat of my own." I bent and retrieved my shoulder bag, the handle of my carry on. "Did I tell you? I rented a place up north, little town called Zephyr. Four whole weeks, starting next week. Just me and the beach and gin and all the clearing I can handle."

Lou Ellen smiled at me. "That sounds like Heaven," she said. "You deserve it, Seph. I hope you have a fantastic time."

As we boarded the ferry, I was surprised to find the ginger cat sitting on one of the benches, staring at us. Lou Ellen let out a low cry and sat next to her, the striped beauty instantly rubbing her cheek against my friend's hand.

"Looks like someone's tired of mice," I said.

"Thanks for saving the day, miss."

The cat looked up at me, winked one amber eye, then went back to her purring and scratches while the ferry's mournful horn sounded and carried us back home.

All was well that ended well. So why then was I suddenly fighting off goosebumps and the odd premonition that I'd somehow opened Pandora's box?

A PERSEPONE PRINGLE COZY MYSTERY

TEN HOARDS A-REAPING

PATTI LARSEN

TEN HOARDS A-REAPING

CHAPTER ONE

My boots crunched over the skiff of fresh snow that still lined the path into the park, the cloudy sky overhead threatening more, crisp scent on the chill air a perfect pairing to the happy counterpoint of the holiday market stalls. I loved this time of year, early December so full of joy and promise, Thanksgiving already over and done with and the rest of the holiday season stretching out toward the turn of the calendar. There was something purely delightful about wrapping up the old and heading into the new, something that had been a constant for me this year in particular. The fact I'd been encountering a lot of firsts over the past six months since my divorce was finalized had me relishing in the experiences as they came and went.

My parting from my husband of over twenty years was amicable and my decision helped a great deal. I had friends who'd endured far worse when their partnerships had dissolved, so I knew just how lucky I was things had gone the way they did. Clean, with caring on both sides and our beautiful daughter, Calliope, fully on board, all meant my newfound singlehood wasn't the sad affair it could certainly have been. I inhaled a deep, fresh breath of air as I passed the first white and red striped tent, the taste of cinnamon and pine now in the back of my throat from the bakery selling delicious treats making me pause and consider taking home some of the sticky buns I loved so much.

"Mom!" I looked away from the lure of the treats to smile at the two young women approaching at a hurried walk, arm in arm. My daughter and her best friend couldn't have been more different in appearance. Calliope's round cheeks and curly light brown hair, not to mention her short and stocky build, were all courtesy of her father, as were her wide, hazel eyes. In stark contrast, Thalia Vesterville, the recent heiress to the massive Vesterville fortune and new mistress of the manor house, tended toward pale and ethereal, her long, blonde hair almost white, blue eyes so light they seemed translucent. Since Thalia's inheritance of her family's estate and affairs, Calliope had been living with her in the massive manor house, something that still concerned me. The two of them rattling around that giant stone mansion, with its echoes of old hurt and discontent, still had me making up unnecessary stories about the influence the pile of brick, wood and ancient history could have on them. Silly, really. They were obviously very happy and Thalia's bright smile when she hugged me matched my daughter's.

"I didn't know you two were coming to this today." Not that I hadn't asked, though I'd made the trek alone, another chance to do something on my list of firsts.

"Last minute decision," Calliope said, hugging me in turn. She looked up at Thalia with a grin pulling her full lips askew. "Lia wanted to get something for Dad for Christmas even though he said he didn't want a gift."

I suppressed the lone twinge I'd felt to this point, and let it go. Holistic therapist or not, I'd been known not to take my own advice a time or two, but this wasn't one of them. Because my single regret in my series of firsts? The fact that Calliope had already informed me she planned to spend Christmas Day with her father, since, according to her, he needed her more than I did.

Fair enough. Never mind he'd also had her for Thanksgiving. Grumble.

"Just something small," Thalia said, her soft voice chiding as her huge eyes met mine. "I can't show up without a gift."

I patted her hand and nodded. "It's very sweet of you." I was already sorting through the resentment and shedding it as quickly as it came. Because Calliope was right. Trent wasn't handling singlehood as well as I was. And there would be other Christmases, other holiday seasons. Besides, I had some big plans for myself for the holidays that were only possible because my daughter chose her father over me.

Oh, dear. Not so over it, after all.

Calliope must have seen it in my face because hers immediately fell. "Mom, maybe we should do a family Christmas this year." She looked up at Thalia again, her friend's expression suddenly concerned as well. "I don't want you to be alone."

That stiffened my spine and had me moving immediately. I hooked arms with both girls and drew them along, away from the seduction of sweets and deeper into the market, smiling until it felt real.

"I'm making my own new traditions this year," I said as brightly as I could, and meant it. "I'm making curry for me, and I bought Bella an expensive piece of salmon." My fluffy white therapy cat, Belladonna, was the joy of my life and of my clients and she deserved a nice feast herself. "I picked up my favorite gin and I plan to drink the whole bottle all by myself."

Thalia giggled. "Callie told me you've been buying yourself things." She let out a soft sigh, contented as she leaned into me while we strolled to the next booth in the line. "That's lovely, Seph."

I nodded, beaming now, wishing I could snag the adorable black knit hat she'd chosen to wear, fur bobble wobbling, instead of the stylish and not really very warm beret I'd chosen to cap my blonde pixie cut. Style over comfort, you betcha. Hey, I was on my own, and looking good was suddenly a priority, thanks. "I've been picking up little things for months," I said, "and tucking them away. I forget most of what I bought." The back of my walk-in closet was a nest of boxes, bags and packages. "I'm going to open them all Christmas morning and have a fantastic time doing it."

"No turkey?" Calliope wrinkled her button nose, stopping to sniff a candle before waving to the vendor and carrying on. The sun broke through the clouds a moment, lighting her hair with hints of gold and red. "What's Christmas without turkey, Mom?"

"Cherise invited me over for some if I decide I want it," I said. My dear friend, Wallace town Sheriff Cherise King, had made the offer as soon as she heard Calliope was going to Trent's for both holidays, but I'd turned her down. I loved her and her family, but sympathy dinner wasn't on the menu for Persephone Pringle's first single Christmas.

"I'm just worried about you." Calliope stopped and squeezed my hand, Thalia pausing as well. They were so beautiful, both of them, I could barely stand it, wanting to hug them all over again and never let them go.

"I have everything I need," I said, touching her round cheek with my gloved fingertips before pulling her to me and squeezing her so hard she squeaked.

"Love you, Mom," she whispered.

"Love you, too," I whispered back.

I wished that moment could have lasted forever. But as was always the case, time held its breath for no woman and a moment later my daughter pulled away, eyes wide as she crossed to a booth with excited strides. I joined her, Thalia leaning in beside her, admiring the collection of blown glass ornaments, each one depicting one of the twelve days of Christmas. I was about to lift one of the delicate balls into my hand to examine the contents when someone stopped at my side. I looked up immediately into the smiling face of Justin Perrier. His grin spread as I smiled in return, giving the young man a curious up and down and raising an eyebrow at his very official-looking uniform.

"Hey, Ms. P," he said in his warm and sunny tenor. I didn't miss the side-eye he gave Thalia, and nor was I surprised by the glance he gave her. He'd been trying to get her to agree to date him since tenth grade and never succeeded. I'd always thought him rather sweet and, though a celebrated athlete, not the cruel jock type that he could have been stereotyped into.

"Justin, so nice to see you." I nodded to the security guard badge on his chest as he puffed up just enough inside his dark blue uniform coat to show it off. "I figured you'd be in the academy by now." He'd invited Trent for coffee once to talk about the Bureau and I knew my ex suggested he spend a few years as a beat cop first to give him some experience before applying to Quantico.

Justin's face fell a little, but he covered it well. "I got a bit behind," he said. "Money's tight. Mom's been sick." I'd heard that, yes, and offered my sympathy but he shook it off with that boyish grin returning. "All good. I'm waiting to hear from the state police academy. Pretty sure I'm a shoo-in."

"They'll be lucky to have you," I said. "In the meantime, you're getting a taste of the job, I take it?"

"Just private security for a few places and events around town," he said, turning to show me his hip.

"Taser, no gun." He sounded so disappointed I almost laughed.

"I imagine that will change very quickly," I said.

Justin winked. "Excuse me, Ms. P. Going to say hi to Thalia." It was obvious then he'd used me as an opportunity to do just that and I let him go, shaking my head. Whatever made him think she'd change her mind, that was on Justin, though she'd told me when I'd asked once he'd never been inappropriate or bullying. Whatever reason she had for saying no, that was between them.

I sighed over young love—and lack thereof, ready to move on. Except, as I turned to do just that, someone jostled me, the impact spinning me around.

CHAPTER TWO

The culprit was a young woman who immediately muttered an apology, but it wasn't her words that caught my attention. The tears in her eyes, one trickling down her cheek, had me catching her hand before she could hurry away.

"I'm fine," I said in my best therapist voice, letting her see my empathy on my face. That might sound contrived, but I'd spent the bulk of my adult life tending to the emotional and mental health of others, so it came naturally. "Are you all right?"

She blinked at me, her dark eyes wide, full lower lip trembling as another tear spilled down over her round, pink cheek. It appeared she was at the beginning of her upset, her face flushing slowly, breath inhaling in a sharp and jerking hitch as she shook her head, tucking her blue mittens under the arms of her matching wool coat. "I'm just… looking for someone. Excuse me." She rushed off then, her dark ponytail swinging behind her as she disappeared into the growing crowd lining the walkway between stalls. I almost turned away but caught sight of her one more time as a few of the shoppers parted, seeing her stop beside a large, white-bearded man near the center of the setup. He paused as she spoke to him, a giant candy-cane in his hands. But before the girl could say much, a small, wiry woman in an elf costume placed herself between them. I couldn't hear what was said but it was obvious to me Santa's helper wasn't in the best mood.

"Hot chocolate?" I spun in surprise to find Cherise standing behind me, smiling down at me as she held out a paper cup. I took it automatically, glancing toward the drama unfolding again, only to find the crowd had closed in and my line of sight was gone.

"Thank you," I said, sipping the drink, a marshmallow bobbing to block the small hole in the lid.

She nodded, her close-cropped black curls hidden under a tight wool cap, tall, Amazonian body impressive in her long, black coat and denims, her characteristic cowboy boots not the smartest footwear for snow but not my choice to make. Her perfect teeth flashed against her dark skin as she nodded to the girls who turned to say hello before returning their attention to the ornaments they seemed obsessed over.

"Spotted you coming in," Cherise said, her gaze skimming the crowd before returning to me. She might have looked casual on the outside, but like me and my years in therapy, Cherise King's training and experience as a homicide detective in Chicago translated to her particular habit of watchfulness that I was now used to and expected from her. Wallace, Maine might have been a sleepy and quiet burg on the Atlantic Ocean, but to our sheriff nowhere was entirely safe, and keeping an eye out for trouble was second nature. "You change your mind about dinner at my house yet?"

I licked the foam from the melting marshmallow from my upper lip and shook my head, grinning. "You change your mind about joining me for gin and curry yet?"

Cherise let out a long, soft sigh. "Girl, don't tempt me." She laughed a little. "I love Martin and the kids, but what I wouldn't give for a day to myself." She shook her head and shrugged, smile soft. "You know the offer's open."

I was about to assure her I was fine—wasn't I?—when she stiffened slightly. Not a lot, not so much anyone else might notice, but I was used to her and her tells, had trained myself to watch for subtleties. So, when our moment of chatting was interrupted by a strange woman I'd never met, I wasn't surprised by her sudden arrival.

"Sheriff King." The tall, slim woman in the long black coat ignored me completely, sticking her gloved hand out and shaking Cherise's when my friend slowly responded. The woman let the sheriff's hand fall quickly, her attitude impatient, words clipped and fast as she spoke again. "SA Gabriella

Savoy, FBI." She flashed a badge that had me frowning and Cherise examining it before my friend nodded.

"What can I do for you, Agent Savoy?" Cherise's tone had changed, filling out, dropping a half a note or so, from casual kindness to professional in a heartbeat.

The agent glanced at me, her hazel eyes meeting mine, pinched nose and lean face almost too drawn for good health. She was pale, like Thalia, but without the vitality of the younger woman, obvious anxiety, and some other mental demon holding her rigid. I took in her tightly bound dark hair, the ponytail almost severe, and the way she held her lean form inside her black suit and long coat as though she might break if she allowed herself to bend and immediately placed her in the *too wound up for her own good* category.

I'd seen Trent in such a state enough times to recognize it was work-related. My FBI Agent In Charge ex-husband had learned to deal with it, but Agent Savoy obviously hadn't yet.

"Can we talk alone, please? This is about that case I called about." Savoy looked away from me, back to Cherise, who shrugged so casually that if I didn't know better, I'd think she was mocking the agent.

"Ms. Pringle is an associate," Cherise said, surprising me. Then again, we'd worked on a murder investigation together before and I would have bet she recognized the issues with the agent as well. My particular expertise did come in handy, though I didn't know Cherise to have anything against anyone from the Bureau. After all, she was Trent's friend before she was mine, and remained so, even if he claimed I'd poached her from him.

Savoy hesitated then shrugged herself, though hers hitched her already tense shoulders up almost to her ears and back again in a sharp motion that had me worried about her even more. "You reviewed the file?"

"I did," Cherise said. Ah, so the sheriff already knew what was going on and still wanted me here. Okay, time to pay closer attention. "You suspect a theft plot is in progress for Wallace."

"A jewelry heist," Savoy said, lowering her voice, nodding. "Wouldn't we be better served having this conversation at your office?"

Cherise exhaled a heavy gust, shaking her head. "I'm not convinced, Agent Savoy."

The FBI agent tsked softly under her breath, body jerking with tension. "If you actually reviewed my notes," she snarled through clenched teeth, "you'd have seen the pattern of thefts occurs every holiday season, Sheriff King, through small towns just like this one. Twelve targets, twelve heists, over six weeks."

"I'm not debating your information," Cherise said in her calm and steady voice. "I am debating your intel."

"I have it on good authority Wallace might be next." Savoy was clearly devolving into anger, voice rising in the face of Cherise's cooler demeanor.

"There are any number of towns on your list,"

Cherise answered her.

Savoy's teeth actually ground together before she shoved both hands so far down into her coat pockets that they stretched the wool over her shoulders. "Not according to my contact," she said.

I was surprised by the sheriff's attitude, truth be told. Surely, such a threat, even if only a chance of one, was something she needed to pay close attention to. It wasn't like Cherise to ignore an early warning. Something was definitely up, and I didn't have sufficient information to make a judgment either way. I did, however, trust Cherise implicitly, especially as I watched the agent spiral into an emotional state. I didn't judge her for that, either, but it was obvious this was personal to Savoy in some way and that was never a good place to come to an investigation from.

Whatever counter Cherise had in mind—and why she was arguing in the first place—was going to have to wait. Because, as the sheriff drew a breath to counter Savoy, we were joined by yet another stranger, this one far less inclined to keep things on the down low than the agent had been.

"Well, *finally*," he huffed, long, thin nose bright pink in the chill of the air, sunken dark eyes fixing Savoy with a furious stare as he looked down that impressive schnoz at her. "Agent Savoy, I've been looking *everywhere* for you."

She instantly stiffened but didn't look his way. "I'll be right with you, Mr. Adams," she said.

"You'll deal with me this *instant*," he snapped back, lean body lurching forward, camel-colored wool coat swinging as he grabbed her arm. "Your incompetence and complete lack of anything resembling investigative ability allowed someone to abscond with my merchandise three days ago and I want to know just what it is you're doing about it."

CHAPTER THREE

Cherise interrupted before the agent could respond to the man's accusation.

"Sheriff King," she said, offering her hand to him while he spun on her, distracted at last by her presence. He spluttered a moment before shaking hers, dark eyes snapping rage.

"Sheriff," he said. "Thompson Adams, Fine Line Brokerage." He handed her a card which she accepted immediately, glancing at it before handing it to me in a casual pass-off. I skimmed it, took note of his ownership of the firm, and returned it to her while he went on. "I supply fine gems and jewelry to this part of the Eastern seaboard." He jabbed a finger at Savoy. "Despite the best efforts of Agent Savoy and the FBI," his entire tone and attitude said exactly what he felt about her and the Bureau in general in the most derisive way possible, "she has continually disappointed." Youch, that was brutal and unnecessary. Then again… "I've requested other assistance countless times, but I'm always stuck with *her*." He sniffed like her very presence offended him. "I'm frankly sick of it."

Savoy didn't respond to his verbal attack, scowling at Cherise. "We'll talk later, sheriff," she said before hurrying off. Thompson Adams gurgled something, eyes bulging before he rushed after her, calling for her to stop. I watched her go, the tall, skinny broker chasing her down, while Cherise exhaled again. When I looked back, she was staring into her hot chocolate with a frown of her own.

"Sorry to drag you into that," she said. "I just needed a buffer."

"My pleasure," I said. "She's a bit tightly wound."

"You can say that again." Cherise crossed to the trash can nearby and dumped the rest of her drink, hands tucking into the pockets of her coat. "She's been badgering me for two days now. I keep asking for proof of her intel, but she won't provide it. And while I'm pretty sure she thinks she's right, I can't act unless I have all the info." Cherise's expression settled into a scowl. "Freaking frustrating. I'm going to go chat with Trent. Maybe he can tell me more about her and if I can trust her." Cherise winked at me. "Feds, right?" I winked back. "See you later."

I watched my friend go, finishing my hot chocolate and disposing of the cup, noting that Calliope and Thalia had wandered off a few booths down, totally missing the drama that I'd just been part of. Just as well. I carried on myself, coming to the end of the stalls and turning toward the next in the maze of booths when I spotted a young woman struggling with a giant, red fabric bag. Impulse had me moving to help her as the crowd parted to let her through. She flashed me a smile when I grasped for the bottom of the bag and hoisted it, surprised at how heavy it was.

"Should have emptied the stupid thing before I took it out of the truck," she said. "Thanks for the help."

It was obvious where the bag was intended for and whose it was, the festival Santa's pavilion in the center of the park our clear destination. I could feel the hard edges of boxes inside it as I shifted my grip, the fake presents—or maybe real ones?—within making transport of the bulky bag all the more awkward.

"Then again," I said, "this saves you from having to carry them all in one at a time."

"Tell me about it." We cleared the final booth and stepped onto the fake grass that someone spread out in the center of the space, covering the frozen ground where Santa's tent stood. The red carpet to the throne in the middle and various decorations had transformed the space into a North Pole facsimile, though whoever was in charge of the decorations had decided tacky and plastic was the name of the game. Whatever, the kids would love it and that was all that mattered.

"Right here." The young woman stopped next to the throne and set her end of the bag down and I copied her, accepting her smile of thanks along with her words. "You're the best."

"Persephone Pringle." I shook her hand as she returned the gesture.

"Ivy Bells," she said, eye rolling and laughing as I arched an eyebrow with a grin growing. "Yeah, yeah. I know. Don't even. I've heard it all." She jerked a thumb at the tent behind her. "Dad's a Santa. He thought it was funny." Her soft laugh had an edge to it, though she quickly seemed to smother it, white-mittened hands stuffing her escaping blonde curls back under her red hat. Her matching red coat and denims made her look the Christmas part, believe it.

"I heard Charles was sick," I said. Our usual town Santa, Charles Harper, was advancing in age and, from what the rumor mill told me, had increasing issues with diabetes. That had put his usual gig in question, and now I had the answer. A shame, really. He'd been Santa in Wallace since I was a girl, but I hardly blamed the poor man for his medical misfortune.

"Dad contracts," Ivy shrugged like it was no big deal. "Pretty good gig if you look like he does."

Was it wrong I had a sudden uncharitable thought about our temporary Santa? That my mind immediately connected dots dropped in my lap by Agent Savoy and had me suspicious of a traveling St. Nick who, from the sound of things, made his living in the very season that concerned her going from town to town to put on the red suit and Ho-Ho-Ho his way around the Eastern seaboard?

Maybe while helping himself to something

sparkly and expensive along the way?

"Ivy." The man in question himself stepped out of the tent and caught sight of me, beaming an instant smile and crossing to us. He certainly did look the part, I'd give him that, from his button nose and full, white beard and mustache to his sparkling blue eyes and round cheeks. He slapped both big hands on his full belly and chortled, sounding like he should as well, while he stopped in front of me, bending from his impressive height to fix me with a grin and a nose-boop.

"And have you been a good girl this year?"

I honestly didn't know what to say to that, shocked by the contact and his overall charisma. In fact, I found myself grinning back, despite my mental leap to the uncharitable.

"Dad," Ivy said, dragging out the title with an embarrassed tone to her voice. "Seriously."

He chuckled and offered me his hand. "Nicholas Bells," he said.

"Persephone Pringle," I said. "Good girl."

He scrutinized me for a moment, then nodded. "I'll check my list," he said. Then winked, one finger on the side of his nose. "I'm supposed to be in disguise."

"Sorry, not buying it," I said back with a laugh. "Definitely Santa Claus. You're not fooling anyone."

He belly laughed and nodded while Ivy sighed, clearly over the whole thing but unable to escape it. His hand settled on her shoulder and squeezed while he gestured at the bag.

"We really should get back to work," he said.

"Lovely to meet you, Persephone."

"Mr. Bells?" I turned to find the young woman who'd run into me earlier had returned and realized this was the very man I'd seen her talking to before Cherise interrupted my nosiness. She wasn't crying any longer, but she didn't look any less upset, her voice wavering as she stared up at him.

His whole happy-go-lucky Santa demeanor faded as he gestured to Ivy who was now scowling at the girl. "Let's go." They both turned and headed for the tent, ignoring the young woman who trembled beside me, while I frowned at the sudden shift in tension in the air. But before I could ask the poor thing any questions, Nicholas Bells snapped, "Clear the area," and disappeared into the tent.

He wasn't talking to Ivy, however. Only then did I notice the green-clad elf helper had reappeared, the older woman in the unsightly and ill-fitting outfit hurrying toward us. I recognized her, of course. Helen November had been Santa's elf for as long as Charles Harper was Santa, though as the town's queen of crotchety cantankerousness, I'd never understood the choice.

Not that she gave a flying fig about my opinion or anyone else's. With her pinched and wrinkled face in a disapproving frown and her frizzy white hair barely contained under her bobbing green hat that tinkled with bells as she stomped toward us, Helen was clearly on a mission for Santa, and I was about to be in the way of that mission if I didn't cut and run right then and there.

"You were *told*," she snarled at the girl beside me,

grabbing her arm and jerking on her hard enough the poor young woman stumbled. "Get lost." Helen's eyes met mine, hers snapping as they landed on me. "Santa's village is closed!"

I knew better than to argue, but I couldn't stand watching her manhandle the shaking girl at my side. "Of course," I said, pulling her free of Helen's grasp and guiding her away. She didn't fight me while the ridiculously clad old woman glared at me with furious intent at my intrusion. "Nice seeing you, Helen."

"Elf!" Nicholas's shout had her spinning. He poked his head out of the tent, furious expression not very Santa-like. "Are you done yet or do I have to replace you?"

Helen twitched like he'd struck her. "How dare you!" Her shriek was thin but carried as she shook an index finger at him. "You're just a temp and don't you forget it! I've been Wallace's town elf for thirty years. We'll just see who gets replaced, you charlatan."

"I have my own elf," he shot back.

Helen bit her lower lip, trembling all over. "We'll just see what town council has to say about that." She stormed off, presumably to find someone of authority while Nicholas grunted something and started to withdraw.

"Please," the young woman at my side stammered at him. "I just need a moment."

But he was already gone, though Ivy appeared, facing her down with a flat and angry expression.

"You're not welcome here," she snarled. "Leave

us alone." With that, she jerked the door to the tent shut, leaving the girl beside me to shake and begin to cry all over again.

But when I reached out to comfort her, she pulled away from me, running off. I almost went after her as I spotted Calliope and Thalia at a nearby booth and exhaled the tension that had gathered inside me during this whole horrible encounter.

Not my business. Why then did my mind refuse to stop whirling even as I rejoined the girls?

CHAPTER FOUR

We'd made a full circuit of all the booths in the market before starting at the beginning again. Calliope's favorite shopping experience included seeing everything there was to see before making purchases, she and Thalia discussing what they planned to buy as they walked ahead of me. I was more than happy to trail along behind them and enjoy their company, even peripherally, with nothing else planned for the day. It had brightened into a lovely morning with the clouds no longer threatening snow and with the bulk of the attendees in a glorious mood. I was rather enjoying simply experiencing the market and people-watching at the same time.

Seeing Nicholas Bell berating his daughter, Ivy, rather rudely interrupted my pleasant stroll, though it did remind me to fire off a text to Cherise about my concern. I felt a little better about accusing the man of possible thievery—or someone of his like, considering the time of year and an excellent excuse he'd have to go from town-to-town—after witnessing him corner his own kid outside the Santa tent and say something so horrible to her that she spun and ran off in tears.

Thought of that, Cherise sent back a moment later. *Good call, Seph. I'm looking into just such a scenario to see if I can track anyone in the Santa business who might have been in all the towns in question.*

Well, of course, she was on it already. She was the professional after all. I hung back from Calliope and Thalia as I spotted the young woman from earlier, her tears dried up but her attention and focus no less on Nicholas than it had been. But before she could approach him, Thompson Adams stormed past her. She seemed to second guess her presence there, flinching back from any contact with the hurrying and clearly unhappy broker. Instead of taking the opportunity to approach Nicholas again, she instead chose to turn and leave with her pale face full of anxiety.

I considered going after her, but she was too fast for me and there was no sign of her a moment later. Sighing over my nosiness and need to help—more the latter than the former I told myself regardless of the truth—I joined the girls at the twelve days of Christmas glass booth and waited as Calliope purchased a full set.

"All finished?" They both nodded. "Hot drinks and decorating at my house?"

"And Bella snuggles," Thalia laughed then. She'd

bonded with my cat more than most.

"And Bella snuggles." They joined me at my SUV, the young heiress waving off her driver and climbing in the back seat of my vehicle like she wasn't a multi-gazillionaire but just folks. Well, she'd practically grown up with us, Calliope's best friend since her parents passed when Thalia was just a girl, and Trent and I had always treated her like she was our second kid. I liked to think I contributed to how well Thalia had turned out, especially considering the family she came from.

The Vestervilles were not known for their good nature.

The girls piled into my house, filling the normally quiet space with laughter and music, immediately turning on the sound system and cranking Christmas carols to obnoxious levels. I sang along with more enthusiasm than I expected, Thalia curled up on the sofa with a purring and kneading Belladonna on her lap while Calliope carefully unboxed each of the glass ornaments she'd purchased.

"But honey," I said, "those are yours."

"I bought them for you." She hung each of them on the hooks she'd placed in a circle on the picture window overlooking my back yard. I'd refused to put up a tree this year, relieved not to have the mess and fuss despite Calliope's pout over the missing spruce. "Well, shoot." She frowned at the box in her hands, the tenth one already open and exposed. "This isn't ten lords a leaping." She showed me the interior's six geese in their nests, a mirror to the one she'd already hung. "They must have put it in the wrong box."

Indeed they had, the outside of the container in question clearly stating it was supposed to be ten lords.

To my surprise, her face contracted, tears welling as she sagged a little.

"It's fine, sweetie," I said. "It's such a lovely gift."

"It's the wrong one." She stuffed it back into the box. "I'm sorry, Mom."

Okay, it was pretty clear she wasn't apologizing for the ornament. I hugged her and rocked her a little as the strains of The First Noel began to play.

"I love you," I whispered to her. "You're the most amazing daughter anyone could ever ask for. And you're such a good person, Callie, to know your father needs you more than I do." I let her go, hands gripping her upper arms. I wasn't tall by any means, but she'd never quite sprouted enough to reach my height, her curls a contrast to my cropped blonde pixie, her hazel no match for my gray-blue eyes. But she was my kid, had my heart as much as her father's looks, and I knew she was struggling. "I want you around," I said. "I'll *always* want you around, whenever you have time. But Trent *needs* you." I surprised myself by blinking away tears of my own, hugging her again. She clung to me a moment then nodded against my shoulder.

"Thanks for understanding, Mom," she said, choked up and barely audible past the song's volume. "He might be an FBI agent, but you've always been stronger than him."

She had no idea. I'd never complained openly to her about her father because our problems weren't her problems. But the years I'd spent feeling unloved, unseen, neglected and abandoned, put second to his job and his own priorities had left me with a bitterness toward him that meant I simply couldn't spend another moment in a marriage to him. He was a good person, a great investigator, a respected boss and agent. But he wasn't the kind of husband or partner I needed him to be.

I took the mismarked box from her and forced a smile. "I'll take care of it," I said. "Now, who wants a snack?"

By the time I'd fed the girls and they'd had their fill of carols and Belladonna, it was almost 5PM. I drove them home, dropping them at Vesterville house, heading back to my place past the market. When I realized it was still open, however, I made an impulse decision and pulled in, parking quickly and hurrying toward the vendor's booth with the box in hand, hoping to put a rapid end to Calliope's disappointment. An image of me sending her a photo of the replacement ten lords had me hurrying past the exiting crowd in the now darkness that had fallen over the park, the fairy lights and streetlamps illuminating the walkway past the closing booths.

"I'm so sorry," the woman said as she examined the box. "I don't have any ten lords left right now. But I'll have one here in the morning."

Well, craptastic. I agreed to return and retraced my steps again, now disappointed myself. Head down, a bit cranky, to be honest, I almost missed the sight of Helen November near Santa's tent, only looking up when I heard her voice raised. She had her arms full of ornamental candy canes already used to line the walkway to the throne in the middle of the village, but that burden didn't stop her from her more immediate task. The fact she was again tormenting the young woman who was weeping once more triggered my irritation further and turned me without conscious thought, changing my course toward them. But the girl dashed before I could support her and Helen then tossed her armload to the ground, the canes clanging against one another, before she vanished into the tent, both targets lost.

Now thoroughly annoyed, mostly with myself for allowing it to bother me, I turned back toward the exit. This time, however, when I spotted Agent Savoy lurking, I stopped in my tracks. She must have had the same idea Cherise and I shared. Surely, the thought had crossed her mind before? If so, why not share that with the sheriff? Or maybe she had? Another situation that wasn't mine to worry about.

Whatever the case, when Thompson again cornered the agent and seemed aggressive, I briefly considered coming to her defense but finally let it go. This wasn't my problem.

Time to go home and pour myself a gin.

CHAPTER FIVE

I hadn't planned to message Cherise again, I swear it, but by the time I'd finished my first drink and poured my second, my curiosity got the better of me.

No updates, she sent back. *Listen, thanks for having my back, but let's just call this, okay?*

Right, fine. Minding my own business.

Wouldn't you know, that only added to my irritation from earlier? I finally went to bed early, Belladonna snuggling me, as though sensing my annoyance. I watched a few episodes of a new TV show on my tablet before managing to fall asleep.

I was in much better spirits the next morning when I headed back to the market, a hot cup of coffee in my tummy over a delicious omelet I'd whipped up, the sun shining and the air warm despite the time of year.

I'd thought the place opened at 9AM, only to realize I was a full hour early when I checked the sign at the entry. Well, darn. Though, the fact there was a coffee shop across the park kitty-corner from the parking lot had me quickly striding around the area to feed my caffeine habit. I could easily entertain myself on my phone or watching people while enjoying another java until the market opened at ten, no problem.

No way was I letting my mood from yesterday return, thank you. Except, as I turned to circle the park and the line of booths, I spotted the young woman from the day before, the one who seemed so desperate to talk to Nicholas Bells, exiting the tent. Without a crowd between us, it was easy to watch her rush out onto the fake grass then hurry toward the parking lot. I moved instinctively to catch up with her, but she spotted me.

She froze in place, face as pale as the white fur of her coat collar. Then, she spun and ran off in the other direction. Whatever just happened, she was terrified, the poor thing. And I had a feeling I knew the cause of her fear. While normally my Momma Bear only showed up for Calliope and Thalia, the poor girl seemed to have the whole world against her, and I'd had it up to my perky blonde pixie cut with the likes of Helen November bullying those who couldn't defend themselves.

Sure, I should have stayed out of it. In hindsight, any rational person would have. But I guess I was still wound up from the night before, frustrated by my own need to be strong so Trent could have a happy Christmas, how Calliope was caught in the middle. Yes, I admit it, as much as I told myself I was looking forward to new traditions, enough resentment toward my ex lingered that I knew I was being influenced by all kinds of layers of irritation.

And that meant emotional reactivity to a totally arbitrary circumstance that I really wasn't meant to be part of.

So be it.

Except, as I strode through the flap of the tent, pushing it aside to confront Helen, I was forced to pause and blink in the dim light, coming in out of the bright sun as I'd done, my gaze falling to a pair of black boots lying on the ground. The soles faced me, toes to the sky, the wearer stretched out behind them, still and silent.

I knew the moment I caught my breath that Nicholas Bells had slung his last sack of gifts.

Santa Claus was dead.

Cherise didn't say a word as I filled her in on why it was that I'd stumbled over the dead body. Bless her, she didn't give me a moment of grief as I told her everything I'd seen and what I knew. Not much, not really, though when I again brought up the possibility that he was the thief, she sighed and closed her notebook.

"It certainly seems relevant." I huddled inside my coat as she observed the local coroner, Owen

Graves, while he examined the body. Dark curls poked out of the elastic hood of his white coverall, light reflecting from his goggles as he got to work. Our town's one-man forensics team and coroner/mortician/medical student might have been twenty-three, but he'd more than proved himself. I know I trusted his judgment. Anyone who could ace the forensics program in two years while studying medicine full-time and helping run his family's mortuary wasn't just a hard worker, he was a natural. Owen stood and staggered a little, apologizing to the deputy standing near him as he bumped the uniform. Okay, he was brilliant *and* a little awkward. No one was perfect.

Owen joined us, nodding to me, pulling his goggles free and pushing back the hood with a swishing sound, the scent of antiseptic heavy around him as he wriggled his freckled nose. "Hey, boss," he said, "Seph." He didn't wait for us to acknowledge him, turning to nod at the body now being zipped up into a bag for transport. The two EMTs made short work of the job. "Time of death is pretty easy to gauge. Liver temp puts it at less than an hour ago." Right around the time I'd seen the upset young woman leave the tent and subsequently found the corpse. "Cause of death is just as easy. Blunt force trauma, some narrow weapon, about and inch in diameter." He raised one gloved hand and brought it down on nothing, as though a demonstration was necessary. "No sign of an obvious murder weapon. You might want your guys to do a sweep. Unless you want me to do it?"

Cherise shook her head. "I'd rather you focused on the autopsy," she said. "They're trained to survey a scene. I'll make sure they're thorough."

"If you need anything, let me know." Owen paused, smiled shyly at me. "Say hi to Callie for me, okay?" And then he was gone, following the gurney out through the tent's main flap, stripping his coveralls as he went.

"The girl," I said as quietly as I could, knowing Cherise would understand my meaning since I'd just told her what I'd seen.

"And Ivy Bells," the sheriff said. "Both girls were here, Seph. But did both have motive?" She exhaled slowly. "A blow to the head like that isn't premeditated. It's a crime of passion, in the moment." I had to agree. And the mysterious young woman's continual upset certainly qualified. Then again, I'd witnessed Nicholas rendering his own daughter to tears, so Ivy might have her reasons, too. But without more information that was all guesswork and really inappropriate, right? "Hopefully my deputies will find the murder weapon shortly and we can print it. Until then, we'll have to sit tight."

Cherise's deputies were already quietly and carefully examining the scene, so there was nothing else for me to do. I was about to turn and go, the small box in my hand reminding me why I'd come in the first place, the mismarked ornament almost forgotten in the drama. But my quick exit wasn't meant to be. An outcry from just past the tent's flap took precedence, Ivy Bells pushing her way through despite the attempt of Cherise's officer to keep her out of the way.

"Dad!" She struggled to keep her feet, staggering into me and I caught her, the small box I still bore falling to my feet. I winced at the thought it might have broken while holding Ivy up, kicking it out of the way for the time being in favor of assisting the grieving girl. Cherise grasped her elbow for extra support, her dark eyes meeting mine before she spoke.

"Ms. Bells," the sheriff said in her kind but professional tone, "I'm so sorry for your loss."

"This can't be happening." Ivy crumbled as I guided her away from the sheriff to sit her down on a large wooden box, closing the lid on a variety of decorations so the girl could rest there. I looked up and spotted Helen November slipping through a flap in the back of the tent, her eyes huge, skinny body rigid inside her elf suit.

Clearly, the space wasn't all that secure, and surely anyone could have had access. I couldn't help but be reminded of the horror on the other girl's face, however, as I pondered the possibility that she'd killed Nicholas herself. One thing was very clear to me. Cherise needed to talk to the young woman I'd seen fleeing the scene as much as the victim's weeping daughter who I tried my best to comfort.

The main flap parted, and Agent Savoy entered, with none other than the girl in question in hand. She pushed the young woman forward, stopping next to Cherise, but before she had a chance to say anything, the way opened one last time and Thompson Adam stormed through.

"I've had enough!" He didn't seem to notice the dead body or Cherise or the crying girls—Ivy and the strange young woman—focused instead on his own affairs. "I'm reporting your incompetence to the Bureau, Agent Savoy. I hope you're fired for this disaster!"

"What are you talking about?" She spun on him, her own anger rising. Clearly, the agent was on her own knife's edge because what I knew of the FBI? They trained agents to maintain professionalism and decorum at all costs. I might not have been her therapist, but even the untrained eye would make assumptions. Savoy was having issues that her bosses wouldn't approve of for her to react like that.

"My merchandise," Thompson snarled at her. "Another theft, last night." He jabbed a finger in her chest. "Despite your assurances, someone stole a million in gems and jewelry from one of my stores and I'm holding you personally responsible."

CHAPTER SIX

It was pretty obvious once Cherise and Agent Savoy set about to investigate Nicholas Bells's belongings for the missing jewelry that I'd outstayed my welcome.

"No civilians," the FBI suit snapped at me while I immediately backed off.

Cherise was kinder, of course, because that was my friend's way, but she carefully guided me to the front flap of the tent with a firm hand and a soft *thank you but that's all for now* before retreating back inside and leaving me on the threshold.

Well, I shouldn't have been surprised to be thus escorted, right? Even if the FBI weren't involved, the actual physical investigation had nothing to do with me, despite my lingering bitter reaction I knew better than to give a moment's angst to.

"Ms. P!" I'd forgotten all about Justin Perrier, the

young man joining me, concern on his handsome face, dark hair poking out from under his knit cap, deep brown eyes framed in long lashes blinking quickly as he joined me. "Are you okay? I heard what happened." He tsked without waiting for my response, staring with what looked like longing at the tent flap. "I should have found the body."

"Trust me," I said, one hand on his arm to draw his attention back, "you'll likely see more than your share in your career. Don't be in a hurry."

"It's not that," he said. "Security was my job. You shouldn't have had to stumble over him like that. And whoever killed him did it under my watch." Justin's distress had me hooking an arm with him, leading him away and toward the vendor stall who was the reason I'd come back in the first place.

"None of this is your fault," I said, stopping and turning him at the edge of the make-believe Santa's village, the crunch of cold fake grass under my boots. "Even the most seasoned officers miss things. Believe it." He nodded but didn't look like he was cutting himself much of a break. "I'm fine, and Cherise is taking care of things."

"Was that an FBI agent with her?" So, he still idolized the Bureau, huh? No doubt he'd be chomping at the bit to go to Quantico as soon as he followed Trent's advice, but at least he was doing it right.

"She's investigating," I said, shrugging because I was so far passed impressed, for obvious reasons that had a lot to do with being formerly married to someone just like her. Well, minus the temperament issue. Trent would be the first person to cooly criticize Savoy for losing herself like that at a scene, especially in front of other law enforcement.

"Is there anything I can do?" He hesitated like he considered doing something epically stupid. I knew that look in his eyes. There was no way to stop him. How was I so sure? Because I'd had the bit between my own teeth a time or two—no judging—and was well aware that dissuading someone from taking action wasn't always the best course of action.

But maybe I could direct him instead and keep him out of trouble? Impulse had me suggesting an alternative. "Keep your eyes open," I said. "Let me know if you see anything suspicious." That would a) keep him out of Cherise's hair and b) make him feel needed while c) maybe uncovering something useful. A win-win-win, right?

Justin's enthusiastic nod had me wincing. "Will do, Ms. P." He saluted me before marching off, head on a swivel. I paused, now feeling guilty. Had I created a monster? Oh, whatever. The likelihood that Justin would stumble on anything important was fairly slim and I had other things to think about.

At least I'd used up the hour required for the vendor to make her appearance. Except, as I headed for the table, I realized I no longer had the original ornament. Well, darn it. I'd left it at the crime scene. Oh well. I needed a replacement regardless, so I'd be coughing up for the ten lords, it seemed, and Calliope none the wiser.

When I requested the vendor open the box, explaining the issue, I admit I wasn't as kind as perhaps I normally would have been, extenuating circumstances and dead bodies being as they were, but she took it in stride with a head shake and an apologetic grin.

"Sorry about that," she said, opening another box and checking the contents before showing me the ten tiny men leaping their way around the inside of the glass ball. It set me back more than I expected, but I guess hand-blown art was worth a hundred bucks a shot.

Yikes. What had Calliope been thinking? Part of me hoped Thalia had paid and part of me hoped she didn't because I hadn't raised my daughter to take advantage of her rich friend like that. Nor did I want to consider my kid's guilt pushed her to spend all that money on a silly Christmas set that I honestly didn't need. "How long are you here?" Maybe I could get into the tent and retrieve the other one for a refund. Hey, I wasn't cheap, but neither was the ornament.

"We close at 9PM tonight," the woman said, "after Santa's done."

Good to know, though maybe she hadn't heard Santa was already done.

Too soon?

I accepted the replacement and turned to leave, knowing I wouldn't get anywhere near the tent yet but hoping I could manage a retrieval later. Now determined to put the horrible beginning to my day behind me (even as I understood I'd be mulling over the details of finding the deceased for the rest of the day, no doubt), I was already planning my return to try to find the stupid box I'd dropped. Only to spot the young woman whose continuing presence had led me to find Nicholas's corpse in the first place.

I didn't think, didn't pause to consider the consequences. Instinct had me in motion almost immediately, tumblers of supposition clicking over in my head about as neatly as the ticking of a clock. You have to know I jumped to a conclusion or two of the homicidal, right? Surely, I'm not the only one in this particular instance who drew such a correlation between the girl I'd seen leaving the tent moments before I uncovered the corpse?

And yes, leaping to such conclusions wasn't my favorite way of being, but I'm not judging you, so give me a little credit, yeah?

She didn't run from me this time, seated on a bench near the perimeter of the market, huddled inside her navy wool coat with her mittened hands shoved deep into her pockets and her head down. I caught sight of the tears dripping into her lap, sparkling drops reflecting the morning sunlight as they fell, and slowed my steps to her side before sinking to the wooden slats next to her.

"Persephone Pringle," I said, offering my hand and my business card.

She sniffled in surprise at my appearance but held her place, taking my details with a hesitant hand before squinting at the surface through her tears. "You're a therapist?" Her dark eyes raised to meet mine again, huge and showing every scrap of her vulnerability. Which, naturally, had me softening from the stern determination that brought me to sit next to her in the first place as my training and natural empathy took over.

"We've met a few times already, under tough circumstances," I said. "But I still don't know your name."

"Holly," she whispered, voice cracking while she tucked my card away in her pocket. Something sparkly flashed in the sunlight, gone again under her cuff as she wiped at her running nose and wet cheeks with the back of her mitten. I fished a packet of tissues from my bag—a therapy staple I was never without—and nodded at her flash of a thankful smile that wavered as much as her voice did. She helped herself to a tissue, mittens now piled in a soft mound in her lap, blowing her nose before she finished. "Holly Bells."

Oh. Well, then. "Nicholas was your father," I said.

She bobbed a nod. She'd been in the tent earlier, so there was no need to sugar coat the past tense I used. Holly had already heard and seen the worst. Then again, my mind assumed she knew before I did, right? Wasn't preparing to accuse her of murder part of the reason I'd stomped my way to her side in the first place? The thing was, though, Cherise had her in her grasp and clearly let her go. So, was I totally out of order here? Of course, now I wasn't so sure myself and needed to either back off or see if I could get the girl to talk further and maybe incriminate herself while Holly spoke again without my prompting.

"I know what you're thinking," she whispered over the crumpled wad of used tissues in her hands, as her fingers turned the ball that she'd made of them over and over in her grasp. She had a terrible habit of chewing her nails, it seemed, the nail beds raw and unhappy looking, her left knee bobbing in a fidget that spoke of severe anxiety and stress even without the training I had. Everything about her body language spoke of hurt and nervousness, likely lifelong as she seemed barely able to meet my eyes or speak above a hoarse, low tone. "I just wanted to talk to him. I found him—" She let out a little sob that she instantly suppressed.

"I'm sorry for your loss, Holly," I said. "There seemed to be a lot of conflict between you."

She shrugged like nothing mattered anymore, cheeks bright pink and lower lip trembling. "He abandoned us," she said. "Me and Mom. He never admitted he was my dad. But I have proof." She fished an envelope out of her jacket pocket, the crumpled thing offered to me. I opened it, recognizing the name of the lab on the front, unsurprised to find a paternity test inside confirming that Nicholas Bells was her father. "He didn't want me." That came out in a thin wail that still didn't rise above barely audible. "And now he's dead."

I didn't get to comfort her, looking up at the sight of Cherise approaching with a deputy at her side. While she'd obviously let Holly walk before, that wasn't going to last. The sheriff nodded to me with a grim expression, and while maybe I should have apologized for not minding my own business, I didn't.

So there.

"Holly?" The young woman looked up with a soft gasp, shrinking against me at the sight of the towering sheriff coming to a halt in front of her. "We have more questions, Ms. Bells."

"I didn't do anything wrong." Cherise had already questioned her, and Holly hadn't tried to run when cut loose. Was that a good sign of innocence? Or maybe she was an excellent actress, and I was deluding myself. But I believed her and instantly reacted to protect her, arm going around Holly's shoulders.

"I'm sure the sheriff just needs to eliminate you as a suspect, Holly," I said.

Cherise glared at me for a moment then shrugged, tossing her hands. "Were you aware of your father's illegal activities, Ms. Bells?"

Holly shook her head, though not in denial, face scrunching further as she continued to lean into me. "Mom always said he was no good," she said, "but he's my dad. I just wanted to get to know him. I didn't want anything from him."

"You killed him!" I wasn't expecting Ivy Bells to burst into the conversation and, apparently, neither was Cherise, though one of her deputies was quick to nab her before she could physically assault the cringing girl I supported. Ivy's lunge ended in a furious stance with her arm gripped by the young uniform, though she appeared ready to jerk free and attack Holly at any second. "You killed my father because he refused to accept the lie you tried to hand us. You're *not* my sister and he *wasn't* your dad and you're a *murderer!*" Red-faced and barely coherent wasn't a good look for her, but I understood to a point. It had to have been a shock for Ivy to discover she had a half-sister. Whatever her father had told her, it was clear the girl didn't want to believe it. But had Nicholas known?

As for Holly, she didn't fight back, simply staring at her hands and the rumpled tissues again, clearly defeated while I held out the paternity test to Cherise. The sheriff read it then sighed before handing it over to Ivy.

At first, the other Bells girl refused to look, but when she finally did glance at it, she let out a soft wail of hurt so deep and painful it made me wince. Holly shuddered next to me while Ivy finally pulled free of the deputy, clutching the page in her shaking hands, tears falling to smear the printer ink as she read the truth right in front of her in black and white.

"It can't be true," she whispered, voice cracking. Ivy looked up and, even as she did, as Holly did the same and met her eyes, I saw it. Saw the resemblance between them though they both clearly took after their respective mothers. Nose, jawline, profile, all a match. Even without the paternity test, it was clear they were equally the victim's progeny.

"I think you both need to come with me," Cherise said.

Holly hesitated while Ivy sagged and nodded, the younger sister meeting my eyes with a plea in her gaze.

"I'm happy to come along with you," I said immediately, ignoring the scowl my sheriff friend shot at me. I rose from the bench, pulling Holly up beside me. "Until you can secure a lawyer, that is."

Holly murmured her thanks, following the deputy who gestured for her to go ahead, Ivy falling in beside her. The sisters kept their distance, but I watched them meet gazes and hoped they might at least connect over this horrible circumstance. Surely, something good could come from their father's death?

Cherise, for her part, walked beside me with her hands in her jacket pockets, stopping me at the perimeter of the fake grass. She leaned over me, still frowning, but when she spoke, there was more concern than anger in her voice.

"If this was just me," she said, "you'd be all-in, Seph. But this is a federal case. Savoy can make life miserable for both of us."

"A suspect requested my assistance," I said. "Savoy can be as unhappy about that as she wants to be, but until Holly asks me to step off, I'm part of this." Not to mention the fact I'd found the body, but whatever.

"Fine, just keep your head down." Cherise flashed me a grin full of malice. "And keep me from murdering that woman, if you don't mind? I'd rather not trade my badge for a jail cell because she's got a bee up her butt." I followed her with a bit more confidence, knowing the sheriff's unhappiness had a different target after all, passing through the tent flap one more time and into the dim interior.

Maybe I could find the stupid box.

CHAPTER SEVEN

Savoy stood over the giant candy cane I'd seen Nicholas Bells carrying into the tent the day before, the plastic split open and the contents spilled out onto a table she'd clearly cleared for this purpose. I ignored the pile of decorations discarded without thought in the corner of the tent she'd liberated from the surface of the rickety folding table, instead focusing on the selection of gems and jewelry— some loose, some in boxes with their lids flipped open, some in bags—scattered and being cataloged by the FBI agent via her phone's camera.

She spun as we entered, scowling at me and opening her mouth, no doubt to order me to leave, when Cherise spoke up.

"Ms. Pringle's presence was requested by Ms. Bells," the sheriff said in a firm and level voice. "Until her lawyer can be present."

Holly retreated toward me, Ivy holding her ground next to a deputy while Cherise stepped forward to join Savoy near the haul.

The agent tsked softly under her breath but let it go, instead focusing on Ivy. "You and your father had quite the racket going," she said, gesturing to the find. What was that look the pair traded? Why did it feel like Savoy was warning the girl of something? The obvious threat in her expression had Ivy rigid but unrepentant.

"I have no idea what you're talking about." Ivy's lack of surprise told me otherwise, her disdain for the agent heavier than I expected. Something was going on here that wasn't being spoken out loud.

As for Holly, she seemed only then to realize what was happening, staring in shock at this new discovery.

"What is all that?" She pointed at the table, gaze rising to the agent, then to her half-sister, and finally to me. "What is going on?"

Savoy ignored her questions, instead staring Ivy down. "You can't tell me you weren't complicit," she said. "And now, you're not just going to stand trial for theft, Ms. Bells. You're going down for murder." Ivy flinched but Savoy didn't give her time to deny the accusation, the agent's face twisting in what looked like dark gloating as she jabbed a finger at the young woman. "What happened, Ivy? Did you fight over the proceeds? Was Nicholas about to cut you off?" Disdain took over with enough arrogance in accusation beneath it I totally understood why Cherise felt the way she did about Savoy. The woman had an attitude problem and a federal badge, and she wasn't afraid to throw accusations around. I called that a bully, but that was just me. "I finally have you and you're going away for life."

"This can't be true." Holly had begun to weep, her sister turning toward her despite Savoy's pinned stare. "Did you kill him?"

Ivy's lips pursed tightly, her eyes narrowing before she tossed her head. "Lawyer," she snapped.

The flap swept aside as Thompson Adams strode in, a deputy at his back. But the officer didn't get a chance to do or say anything, the jewelry broker huffing his way toward the table with his face flashing emotion. I spotted Helen November creeping in after the pair, tucking herself into a corner with a baleful stare for me when she caught me watching. But I was too focused on Thompson to care that Helen had made herself at home. Because what I mistook for shock and horror on the broker's face turned to relief, so I clearly misread him as he rushed the last few steps to his merchandise.

"You did it!" He turned to Savoy, settling into grudging gratitude. "Finally."

"You're welcome," she snapped back.

"I spoke too soon." His voice vibrated with dread as he picked up a necklace and held it to the light, fishing a loupe out of his inside pocket, the small, black magnifying device trembling in his fingers. "This can't be right," he spluttered then, tossing the piece to the table before opening a small pouch and spilling out what looked like a variety of diamonds. He examined each quickly, throwing them aside as though they were worthless, panic more and more obvious while Savoy stiffened, now accepting something wasn't right and her victory might not be at hand after all. Solidified when Thompson finally stepped back, cheeks pale and fury apparent. "Fake," he whispered. "All fake. Every single one of them." She gaped while he turned on her. "What is the meaning of this? Where are my real jewels?"

There wasn't much the agent could say at that point, was there? In fact, we all stood in stunned silence as he poured through the entire collection, discarding every single piece one after another until it was obvious something was seriously wrong.

"These are my pieces," he said at last. "I recognize the inventory. But someone has gone to a lot of trouble to swap them out for fakes." He fished a handkerchief out of his inside jacket pocket and dabbed at his upper lip, then his tall forehead, his panic turned to utter horror. And, finally, fury as he spun on Savoy one more time. "How incompetent *are* you?"

I felt Holly shiver next to me and glanced down at her, my rapt attention at this turn of events broken. Something passed over her face that I didn't recognize, and she ducked her head before I could decipher it. Well, she'd just lost her father after being rejected her whole life and discovered both he and her sister were jewel thieves. I suppose indecipherable emotions weren't all that odd. Except, hadn't I seen her dodging Thompson Adams earlier? Or maybe I'd been imagining things?

"Could the merchandise all have been fake initially?" Savoy was grasping, though it wasn't all that outside the realm of possibility. The fact Ivy looked positively sick at the revelation told me she had no idea. Did she kill her father for a bunch of counterfeit jewels?

"Certainly not," Thompson spluttered. "I personally examine and authenticate everything that comes into my brokerage. I have catalogs of all of the items here with photos and serial numbers. This is a disaster." He stepped back a few paces, again dabbing at his face with his handkerchief, hand shaking. "My insurance company will never believe it. I'm out almost a million dollars because you can't seem to do your job, Agent Savoy." He spun on Ivy before the FBI agent could protest, rage flashing into view. He lunged at her and had her arms in his hands, shaking her, before anyone could react in time. It only took a moment for one of the deputies to separate them, Cherise stepping in personally to pull the furious broker back, but not before he rattled the young woman's teeth together. "What did you do with my merchandise?"

"I didn't do anything!" He wasn't the only one in panic mode, Ivy now shaking violently without his help. She hugged herself tightly, cheeks bright red, tears in her eyes. "I swear, I don't know where the real jewels are."

"But you took these," Cherise said, pointing to the table.

Ivy stared back, mute and rigid, still unwilling to incriminate herself.

"And where are the rest?" Thompson prodded the pile with a furious finger. "These are from the heist last night but we both know there's been more than this stolen, Agent Savoy. The previous night's theft comes to mind. And I'm not the only broker who's been left high and dry."

"We're on it," she snarled through clenched teeth.

"So you've been saying for several years now." He stressed that with so much vitriol she flinched. "I can't believe you still have your job."

To my surprise, Holly spoke up, interrupting. "Even if you can prove my sister stole those," she said in a voice that held more strength than I gave her credit for, "they're fake." Everyone stared at her, including me. Clearly, her mind had been working while the broker and agent had been arguing, locked on the only other person in the tent who meant anything to her. "That's a misdemeanor, right?" She met my eyes, hers hard and angry. "They can't be worth much."

Ivy seemed shocked Holly spoke up for her, and so was I. The young woman had rejected Holly from day one, as had Nicholas. What changed? As for Ivy, she instantly nodded, her own jaw tightening as she faced Savoy and Cherise down. "Holly's right," she said. "You've got squat. And I still don't see my lawyer anywhere around here."

Savoy lurched as though prepared to go after Ivy Bells herself, but Cherise was faster and calmer, putting herself between the young woman and the agent.

"Take her to the office," the sheriff told her deputy. "Ms. Bells's lawyer should be on his way." She nodded then to Holly. "Both Ms. Bells, if you please. While Agent Savoy and I have a conversation about where to go from here."

Yeah, I wouldn't have wanted to be Savoy at that moment. Cherise didn't like feeling foolish and this was turning into a real crap show.

The deputy nodded, escorting the first young woman away. I didn't miss the look that passed between the sisters, the short, almost imperceptible nod from Ivy, the flicker of a smile from Holly, appearing and disappearing so fast I was sure I was the only one who caught both.

Which had me instantly wondering if there was a conspiracy here that I'd missed, and I was being played for a patsy. Well, one way to find out.

"I'm going with you," I said, arm hooked through Holly's, waving off the second deputy moving to do Cherise's bidding.

She seemed relieved and nodded. "Thank you, Ms. Pringle," she said.

We'd see if she'd be thanking me in the end, but either way, I was getting to the bottom of this whether Savoy liked it or not.

CHAPTER EIGHT

We were exiting the tent when Helen November made her presence known, startling me when she lunged for the sheriff and spoke in her shrill voice.

"There's no Santa!" She said what now? Cherise and I both paused to stare. The small woman practically hopped up and down on both feet, face scrunched as tears trickled down her cheeks. "This is a *disaster*." She pulled the bell-laden hat from her thin, white hair and wrung it between both hands, the tinkling a counterpoint to her distress. "*What* are we going to *do?*"

Um, that was the least of our worries, actually, though apparently not so for the town's elf.

"I'm sure the council will think of something." Cherise patted her gently on the shoulder before gesturing for me to leave. I did, shaking my head that the woman even brought up the fact. A man was dead, a million in jewelry stolen, and just in this robbery. And she was worried about who was going to lie to the kids of Wallace about whether there was really a Santa Claus?

Yeah, I might have been a bit cynical by that point. But it wasn't lost on me that trauma was kind of my job, right?

I let the deputies go ahead of me with the girls, glancing back to see Helen fussing with the candy canes lining the walkway to the throne. I waited for a moment before joining her, seeing the tears dripping from her cheeks as she angrily adjusted one of the tall, painted decorations, jerking it out of the ground with a grunt only to move it three inches and drive it into the cold dirt again. I approached her, giving her time to pull herself together when she spotted me, even as someone waved at me from across the way. I waved back at Justin Perrier before returning my attention to Helen.

She straightened her skinny shoulders, the baggy green suit she wore rather comical, even more so with the matching shoes and hat and mittens, all jingling with little bells. There was nothing funny about her expression, however, as she smeared her tears from her cheeks and faced me down.

"This is horrible," she said. "I can't believe Christmas is going to be ruined."

"Everything will be fine, Helen," I said. "There's time to find another Santa."

"You have no idea what you're talking about." She yanked free another candy cane, jabbing the ground with it three inches ahead. Even I could tell she was fighting a losing game. There was no way to line up the decorations with one another in perfect formation. And not just because she was doing it by eye, either, but due to the uneven number. Poor thing, and yet I struggled to empathize with her when she snarled at me. "I told the council this wasn't going to work out. But did they listen to me? *Their* elf? No!" She sniffled and moved to the next candy cane. "I've only been Wallace's elf for the last four decades. Don't pay attention to anything *I* say."

There wasn't much I could do to console her, that much was apparent. And Justin's lingering nearby had me distracted. When he caught my eye, he nodded and tilted his head to the left, before heading in that direction.

"Let me know if I can help." That was about the lamest thing I could have said at the moment, but I was now remembering the conversation I'd had with and was now nervous he'd done something he shouldn't have to prove himself. I'd told him to keep his eyes open and let me know if he'd seen anything. So I could have been catastrophizing, naturally. But the idea he'd either stepped outside the boundaries of what was smart or, better yet, had information Cherise needed to hear, seemed more important than the rage-filled old woman who obviously didn't want my help.

To prove that point, Helen turned her back on me, leaving me no option. With a tinge of guilt over abandoning her smothered by the fear the hens coming home to roost in my attempt to keep Justin from getting in Cherise's way, I left the furiously swearing woman to her task and moved on.

Best laid plans, Seph.

Justin had stopped near one of the vendors, waiting for me, head down, hands in his pockets and when I stopped in front of him, he immediately began to whisper.

"I know it's probably nothing," he said, leaning in to keep the conversation between us, "but I saw that FBI Agent arguing with the victim's daughter earlier." Holly? "It looked like they were really going at it." He shook his head, frowning. "I didn't get to hear what they were talking about, but the girl, Ivy?" Huh, wrong daughter assumption, Seph. "She said something about a deal."

Did she now? What kind of deal might that be? Maybe I wasn't losing my touch about reading people. I'd been struggling with the impression Ivy and Savoy were hiding something. This proved I was right, if not the details. "Thanks, Justin," I said, meaning it. "Great job." He really did have a head for investigating, it seemed.

The relief on his face had me grinning back. "Thanks, Ms. P," he said. "I'll keep watching." I let him go, his shoulders now back and steps easy and I knew I had done the right thing after all.

And maybe he'd actually uncovered something that needed an answer.

I was almost to my SUV, the girls being guided into the back seat of a squad car, when my phone pinged. Imagine my surprise when the text I read was from none other than my ex-husband.

Can't reach Cherise, Trent sent. *I assume you're with*

her. Can you get her to call me?

Is this about the case? I fired that off as I paused to wait for the sheriff to join me. She'd stopped in her tracks just outside the boundary to the parking lot and was talking closely with Savoy. It appeared to me from the distance that the agent was on the verge of hysterics and doing a terrible job of hiding it. From Cherise's stiff and hands-on-hips stance, she was about ready to walk off and never mind what the agent wanted.

Just have her call me, Seph. I eye-rolled at my ex's return text but did as I was told, crossing the distance to Cherise who looked up as I joined them. Savoy stopped talking immediately and stalked off toward her own black SUV, following the squad cars and the girls while Helen November watched with her pinched face pale and tiny body shaking before she scuttled back to Santa's tent and disappeared in the crowd.

"Trent wants you to call him," I said, doing my best to keep the droll irritation from my voice at being a messenger girl. While my ex and I were amicable, we weren't really friends. In fact, the whole reason we divorced was the fact that despite our long life together, the truth remained we had very little in common and friendship just wasn't on the agenda.

"Crap." Cherise checked her phone, muttering another more aggressive swear under her voice as she realized the dark screen wasn't a good sign. "I forgot to charge it last night." She tucked it away and nodded toward mine, still in my hand. "Do you mind?

I certainly didn't and chose his speed dial while grinning impishly at her. She didn't try to take it, letting me put it on speaker as Trent answered.

"Sorry," she said immediately. "Phone's dead. What's up?"

"Seph's listening, isn't she?" He sighed because he knew me well enough, at least. "Listen, it's about Agent Savoy."

The plot thickened. "What about her?" Cherise didn't bother to try to hide her annoyance with his coworker. But wait, hadn't she gone to talk to him yesterday?

"So, she *is* there." He sounded irritated himself. "I'm out of state on a case." Ah, so Cherise's attempt to find out the truth hadn't panned out until now. "But I'm sending agents to escort her out of Wallace."

Well, well, well. "What does that mean?" I met Cherise's gaze when I spoke.

"She's not officially part of the investigation anymore." I knew my ex well enough to hear the disapproval in Trent's calm tone. He'd mastered it over the years as an agent himself, had turned it into a fine-tuned weapon since becoming a Special Agent in Charge. The last time he used it on me, I'd asked for a divorce, so.

Yeah. Might have triggered me a little.

"Just do your best to rein her in," he said, obviously speaking to Cherise. "My people will be there by this evening."

"Understood," Cherise said while inside I burned with need to know.

I hung up without saying goodbye, arching an eyebrow at my friend. "You're not going to leave it at that, right?"

She flashed me a grin so tight and vicious I almost laughed. "Let's have a little chat with Agent Savoy."

We caught up with her at the office, Cherise stopping her as Savoy climbed the steps to the front door. I waited with my friend, observing behavior (snort, nosy, yeah, I know) while the sheriff dealt with Trent's rogue agent.

"I just got a very uncomfortable call from the FBI," Cherise said. Stopped and waited.

To her credit, Savoy nodded, though I could practically see her mind twisting inside her looking for a way around this situation. "I'm not here officially," she said.

"I have FBI agents coming to take over this case," Cherise snapped at her then. My sheriff friend didn't often show her temper—except with her teenage daughter, fair enough—so seeing her crack like that had me concerned. But she quickly pulled herself back under control, voice low and firm, towering from her almost six-foot height over the slim agent. "This is my town, Agent Savoy. My jurisdiction."

"Federal case," the woman said. "Cross-state theft."

"So you say," Cherise shot back. "And yet, the items we retrieved are all from Wallace, yes?" Savoy clearly agonized before nodding once. "I need a really good reason not to send you packing right now."

"This is *my* case," the woman snarled before doing as Cherise had done, jerking herself visibly under control. No empathy, not yet, but I was beginning to have an inkling of her conflict. "I've been chasing Nicholas Bells for three years, sheriff. I can't let this go."

"You knew it was Bells," Cherise said. "Why didn't you say so?"

"No proof." Savoy shook her head, now disgusted all over again, but with herself this time. "I made mistakes, and he was slick. But I had him, sheriff." She glanced at me before deflating somewhat, almost looking defeated. Okay, there was my compassion, if only a little. "My former partner bungled the last arrest attempt and when the whole case fell apart, my bosses pulled me from it and made Jared retire." She jammed her hands into her coat pockets. "I couldn't let it stand."

"I don't care what kind of mess you make outside of my town," Cherise said. "But you brought this to my doorstep, Savoy, and now I have to deal with it." She blew out a loud breath while the agent nodded.

"Ivy Bells killed her father," the agent said then as if nothing had changed. "For the money. I'm sure of it."

"What money?" Cherise tossed her hands. "There *is* no money, no real jewels, just fakes."

"Then Thompson Adams," Savoy lobbed at her, desperation returning. "I'm telling you, there's more going on than I was ever able to uncover."

Cherise might have agreed with her. I know I did,

because there were so many questions and very few answers, but Savoy wasn't the one to uncover the truth and had proved it, no matter what she wanted. Not to mention I now suspected she was hiding something to do with Ivy. I needed to tell Cherise but we'd traveled separately and now I'd lost my chance to do so without Savoy being in the know. "Your bosses at the Bureau told you to step off. I have to believe they had good reason for that." Savoy's jaw jumped but she didn't argue. "Let's face it. You've got nothing, agent. And I have a dead body and only your say-so that the kid did it. Sorry, but I'm not going to trust your judgment at this point. Seph." Cherise gestured abruptly at the door. "After you. Agent Savoy, I suggest you get out of town before your fellow agents arrive. Let's go."

I followed Cherise into reception, glancing back at Savoy over my shoulder. She'd slumped somewhat but stiffened as the door closed and marched off toward her car. It was pretty obvious to me she wasn't about to bail on this case just yet—if ever.

That didn't mean I minded my own business, though. "Cherise." I stopped her before she could enter the bullpen, the tall sheriff turning to face me while deputies wrangled the young women they'd just escorted inside. I had two things to bring up and picked the first one at random. "Thompson Adams?"

Cherise nodded, voice low and quiet. "Dude's sketchy," she admitted. "I'm already looking into him, but from what I've gotten so far, Seph, his rep is impeccable. This is the third time he's had problems with the same thief over three years in three different jurisdictions. And none of the missing jewelry was ever recovered."

"Could they have been fake all along?" I repeated that question while she wrinkled her nose at me.

She didn't get to answer, however, the door sweeping open and Thompson Adams entering in a huff.

"I want Agent Gabriella Savoy arrested," he said.

Cherise's surprise matched my own. "For what?"

"Isn't it obvious?" He stared down his narrow nose at the sheriff like talking to her about this whole mess was beneath him but inescapable. "What better way to hide a crime than to be the one investigating it?" Thompson glanced back and forth between me and the sheriff before nodding once in decisive accusation. "She's been the thief all along."

CHAPTER NINE

That was quite the accusation, though honestly, was it far-fetched? I hadn't come across that idea myself but knew my biases when it came to law enforcement didn't encourage such connections. But could Thompson Adams be right? Was Agent Savoy far more involved than she let on herself? Why else risk her career?

And didn't I already suspect Savoy and Ivy had something between them that wasn't yet revealed? The possibility they were working together wasn't that far of a stretch at the moment.

"Mr. Adams," Cherise said with a stern expression that silenced him but didn't do much else, "I know you've heard this before, but you need to leave the investigation to the police."

"You're right," he snapped. "And I've been disillusioned and let down over and over again,

Sheriff King." He tossed both hands. "I take it you're not even going to consider her as a suspect, are you? Why do I waste my time?" Thompson crossed his arms over his chest in a dramatic fashion that involved his coat swirling and eyebrows arching over his long nose. He paused for effect, glaring at Cherise. "I'll just have to get answers for myself, then."

That was all we needed. One nosy busybody digging in where she didn't belong was enough, right?

"If you're not going to charge me," Ivy called to her over the divider to the bullpen, interrupting before Cherise could shoot the man down (not literally, come on, she wasn't that angry. I don't think, at least) "I demand you let me go, sheriff."

Okay, I winced. I didn't even have to see the look on my friend's face to know the kind of impact Ivy Bells's words had on the sheriff. Already triggered, it was obvious to me Cherise was on the brink of losing what few scraps of control she had left over her temper. That had me worried about my normally stoic and collected friend. It couldn't have been easy to do her job, let alone deal with a rogue FBI agent who was only bringing more drama to the table, not less. I didn't envy her, but I could support her.

You betcha.

"You still have questions to answer, Ms. Bells," Cherise said over her shoulder.

I caught Ivy's rebellious expression, but it was Holly's sadness and fear that had my empathy firmly in place. Then again, why was she trying so hard to hide behind the deputy? And was that fear or nervousness? She seemed reluctant to look up at Thompson Adams. What *was* going on there? I was reminded my instincts had proven at least mostly correct, though if I was right and she had reason to hide from Thompson, her possible guilt meant I wasn't as observant as I thought I was.

"This is ridiculous," Ivy snarled.

"It's going to be all right," Holly whispered, just loud enough for me to hear.

Ivy spun on her, regardless of their previous moment of connection, her fury now turned on her sister. "Shut *up*," she snapped. "This is all your fault."

Holly spluttered, but even as she tried to deny it, I saw her gaze flicker to Thompson even as he perked and jabbed an index finger in her direction.

"Wait," he said. "I know you."

Holly shook her head, tried to back away, but was stopped by the deputy who stood behind her. Ivy took a half step aside fully exposing her younger sister to the broker.

"Ms. Bells?" Cherise turned to the girl who seemed about ready to collapse in on herself at any second, my protectiveness rising but contained since it was obvious that Holly hadn't been entirely forthcoming.

"Bells?" Thompson shook his head. "That's Holly... Roach, isn't it? You worked in one of the stores in Belmont."

Holly stammered a moment, but Ivy leaped on that information.

"See? I had nothing to do with it." She crossed

her arms over her chest, back turned to her sister. "She's in on the whole thing. I'm innocent."

Yeah, I was buying that. Not.

"I didn't do anything." Holly crumpled into a chair, the deputy catching her before she could fall. "I swear. I just wanted to see Dad. I had no idea he was a thief. Mom said he was into shady stuff, but she never told me he was a full-on criminal." She looked up at me. "I swear, I didn't steal anything or hurt anyone."

"Why didn't you disclose you worked in one of the stores that was robbed, Ms. Bells?" Cherise asked before Thompson could accuse the girl of anything. He tsked at the sheriff for the interruption, but my friend's steady gaze returned to him a moment and he finally took the hint and went quiet.

"It was last year," Holly said. "I didn't even know it meant anything. I don't even know what's going *on*." She burst into tears, face cupped in her hands, and I finally moved to join her. She hugged me as I sat next to her, waving off the officer who shrugged and let me take over. "I saw Mr. Adams, how angry he was. I knew if he recognized me he'd accuse me, especially after all this." She tossed her hands. "Please, I have no idea what's happening."

Except, she'd been hiding from him before Nicholas died, so before she supposedly knew he was a thief. "There's more to this, Holly," I said without accusation but enough firmness she caved.

Holly nodded, gulping. "He was horrible to all the girls at the store," she said. "The worst kind of bully. He even got one of my friends fired, claimed she stole property. But she *didn't.*" Holly wiped at her nose aggressively with one wrist, something sparkling quickly before her cuff covered it. It wasn't the first time I'd seen that flash of brilliance, either. "I left the store after the robbery last year. I didn't want anything to do with him or that place ever again."

I wasn't sure she was telling me everything, but I could certainly see Thompson Adams filling the role she just accused him of. Still, it gave me an opening and I took it, despite Cherise's present emotional state.

"Holly," I said. "I saw you coming out of the tent before I found your father's body."

She hitched a breath. "I found him," she whispered. "But I didn't kill him."

"The whole family is crooked." Thompson's derision cut through my kindness and made Holly flinch. "Arrest both girls and sort it out later, sheriff. They're obviously in on it with their thief of a father." He tilted his head, looking down that narrow nose again. "Despicable."

Holly started crying once more, reaching up to wipe at her nose. The sparkle of something again caught my eye and I wasn't the only one. "I swear," she whispered to me, even as Thompson Adams finally made it past Cherise and into the bullpen.

He had his hand around Holly's wrist before I could stop him, jerking on the bracelet she wore. "There, you see?" He pulled it free, the clasp breaking off in his hand. Cherise pulled him away, but the damage was done. "This is one of mine, I'd swear to it." But as he shook it at Holly, his eyes widened, and his raging stilled. "It can't be," he breathed, then stopped, swallowing hard, licking his lips. "Where did you get this?"

Holly's crying had only increased, but I made out, "Dad gave it to me," between sobs. "Last night." She clung to me. "Did he steal it?"

I didn't respond since the answer was pretty obvious at this point.

Except Thompson seemed shaken by the item he'd so aggressively claimed and when he finally handed it to Cherise, it was with a trembling hand.

"It's real," he said. Stopped. Spluttered, then tried to speak again before going silent.

"He said that was all he owed me," Holly said, voice raspy as she caught her hiccupping breath between sobs. "And to get lost."

It was only because I looked up to Cherise that I caught Ivy's reaction, startled that the girl seemed upset by the revelation, though not by the gift. Instead, there was actual empathy on her face, and it almost appeared as though she leaned toward her sister. That had my mind returning to the idea maybe the sisters had more between them than a criminal father.

"No one is going anywhere," Cherise said. "As soon as your lawyer arrives, we'll get things sorted out. Until then, Mr. Adams, I recommend you return to reception and have a seat. I'll be with you shortly."

Thompson spluttered and Thompson protested but, in the end, escorted firmly by a deputy, Thompson retreated, leaving me with Holly and Ivy and a sick feeling in my stomach that maybe I was being played after all.

Wouldn't be the first time.

CHAPTER TEN

I fully expected Cherise to ask me to leave, so I was surprised when she instead pulled me aside.

"I think this might be a good time for Bella to make an appearance," she said, nodding toward the weeping Holly.

"I'll be right back." It was a quick drive home, just a few blocks away. I even remembered to leave the very expensive ornament on the kitchen counter, so go me. I returned immediately with the fluffy white cat I'd adopted just a few months ago in the carrier she despised. Her mournful meowing at being confined quickly turned to purrs as I lifted her out of the lap of luxury and into the startled arms of the crying younger Bells.

Holly hugged the cat to her, Belladonna's trademark rumbling and muttering matched with my darling girl's sweet temperament and seemingly keen sense of people's needs had the young woman quickly relaxing enough that Bella's long, white fur draped over Holly's knees as two paws made biscuits on her jeans.

"She's beautiful," Holly said.

"Belladonna is a dear," I said.

Holly's sniffling had retreated, and I even caught a smile while her once trembling hand softly stroking the cat's fur. "Thank you, Seph," she said. "This helps a lot." A long inhale ended in a shaky exhale but when Holly met my eyes again, Cherise leaning against the desk beside her, the young woman's expression was open and clear at last. "I didn't kill my father," she said. "I didn't have anything to do with his death, with the theft, with the fake jewels. None of it." She looked down again when Bella chirped, realizing her hand had fallen still, starting up the slow and steady strokes again. "This is all a huge mistake. I should have listened to my mother." She hesitated then before turning to Cherise. "He didn't give me that bracelet," she said. "I stole it from him."

"So, you did know he was a thief," my sheriff friend said without a trace of accusation.

Holly sighed deeply one more time, sagging into herself while Belladonna's purr amped up in response. "I did," she said. "Mom warned me." She shook her head then. "I can't believe I did that. Took the bracelet, I mean." Visible regret crossed her face, fresh tears rising in her eyes. "I never wanted to be like him. I just... it was dumb and misguided and I'm really sorry. I was going to return it." She looked back and forth between us, earnest, making me want to believe her in her near-breathless confession. "That's why I was in the tent. I was going to give him the bracelet and leave and never come back." Horror rose in her eyes, her desperation turning to despair in a slow wave of visible emotion that had me wishing I could hug her. "I should have just gone home." Holly began crying again, but there was a catharsis to the sound, not the aching and heavy sobs from before, her body uncoiling from that horrible hurt and settling into acceptance. Belladonna clearly sensed it because she rose and stretched, turning toward Holly and standing up with her paws on the girl's chest, licking her cheek before head-butting her. That made Holly laugh, a choking sound but with genuine amusement as she hugged Bella again. "She really is amazing."

There'd be a nice chunk of fresh salmon for my furgirl when we got home, believe it. And though I knew it was possible Holly was a good enough actress she could be playing me, I found myself believing her story.

Except, she might have been able to fool me, but Bella? She had a knack for sussing out the psychopaths and sociopaths who did their best to hide their true nature. No one fooled Belladonna. No one.

Which had me turning to Ivy who watched the whole thing unfold with a sour expression on her face.

"You're just going to take her word for it?" She seemed surprised by her own words, blanching and looking away as if the guilt that crossed her face wasn't welcome. The way she tightly crossed her arms over her chest immediately identified her regret to my trained eye.

"For now," Cherise said. "Your turn, Ms. Bells."

Before Ivy even spoke again, I caught a flicker of motion and found my gaze turning toward reception and the tight and nervous look on Thompson Adams's face. The man was hiding something. But his turn would come. Though no way was I letting him hold my cat.

Ivy stayed where she was, arms crossed, glaring at Belladonna in her sister's lap but made no move to take advantage of the furry therapy available. Instead, she fixed Cherise with a flat stare and shook her head.

"My lawyer's not here yet," she said.

"Would you rather sit in a cell downstairs?" The sheriff shrugged before Ivy could respond. "Have a seat, Ms. Bells. I'll deal with you when your legal representation arrives." She turned her head, dark eyes meeting mine. "I'll be in my office."

I watched her cross to her door and pass through, though she left it open, sitting at her desk and picking up her phone. It was obvious that she was leaving the girls to me, and why. Cherise might not have been in a position to speak to Ivy without her lawyer present, but I certainly could. Since neither of them were clients of mine and I didn't work for the sheriff's department the rules were gray enough that if I managed to get them to say something out in the open of the office, while maybe inadmissible in court, it could be used to uncover other clues.

I didn't like it, and it left me with an uncomfortable feeling, but a man had died and even if he wasn't a good person morally, even thieves deserved justice when it came to murder.

That had me leaving Holly in Belladonna's tender care while I crossed to Ivy and sat down. She made a soft sound of protest before gusting out a heavy inhale and thudding herself into a wooden seat next to the desk where the deputy had left her. But she refused to budge, to unwind her arms or to look at me, instead staring with determined rebellion at the far wall.

I'd dealt with more than enough of my share of resistant clients sent to me for assessment, so this was hardly a new situation. I knew better than to ask questions, however, just sitting and being still and allowing Ivy the space to come to her own decisions about what she wanted to share.

There's a thing about silence and suspects, you see, a discomfort that arises from not speaking when stress is eating you up inside. And Ivy wasn't immune, was she? I could tell from the way her face twisted, how she chewed the inside of her cheek a few times, the way she twisted in her chair as though she couldn't find a good position to be so rigid in. Time and impatience finally won as she spun on me with a snarl.

"I didn't kill him," she said, hunching down inside her coat, that open rebellion on her face turning to a mix of anger and sadness as she fought off tears, dashing them from her eyes before they could fall then hugging herself again. "He wasn't always an awful dad, you know." I let her vent, nodding just enough to acknowledge her words, keeping my expression soft and open. "Fine, I hated him, are you happy now?" Her outburst wasn't surprising, honestly, so I was able to maintain my composure as I poured all the empathy I could into my being and let her carry on. Ivy grunted as she sank back further into her chair, the wood creaking when she shifted, before she blurted her next tidbit. "I'm the reason that FBI agent is here."

Well, now. I had my own guesses about that and shared the top of the list. "You told her your father was the thief," I said.

Ivy looked away, biting so hard at her lower lip that it turned white, paling out as her eyes welled with tears again. Holly let out a soft sound and stood, Belladonna in her arms, crossing to both of us. She pulled up a chair with one foot before sinking into it next to her sister. My cat stood on the younger woman's lap but stared at Ivy with hooded eyes, purring deeply and steadily as the older sister finally relented her tension and uncrossed her arms. She quickly covered her face, but Holly didn't let her hide, tugging at her sleeve until Ivy released her shield and let both hands thud into her lap.

"I'm sorry," she gushed at Holly, soft sob of her own making her sound even more like her sibling. "I knew all about you. So did Dad. I shouldn't have been so mean. But he said we couldn't let you in, that it was too dangerous. He didn't want anything to do with you." She caught herself as Holly nodded back, her despair now gone, at least, even if Ivy's remained, finally reaching the surface.

"It's okay," Holly said with a teary smile, squeezing Ivy's hand. "It really is."

"None of it is okay," Ivy said, now staring at the floor with vague horror, her ponytail's disarray knotting her fine hair near the nape of her neck, strands wavering with static. "I never wanted to have anything to do with it, but he was my dad." That was aimed at me, through more tears and regret. Now that she'd allowed herself to crack, it seemed everything was ready to pour out and I had no intention of stopping her from carrying on. Especially when I spotted Cherise coming to her door out of the corner of my eye, pausing to listen herself. "I was only fourteen when he started the jewelry heists. Up to then, I was just his lookout, did a bit of shoplifting, nothing big. I only did it because I wanted him to love me."

"I totally understand," I said, Holly nodding with me.

"You have no idea how hard it's been." Ivy wiped at her face with her free hand, but I noted she made no effort to pull away from her sister. The connection that I'd guessed at wasn't some prior knowledge after all. No, from what I could see it was simply two young women who realized they were family and had no one else to look out for them in the here and now. Again, maybe I was wrong, but as Ivy went on, Holly's compassion for her sister matched my own enough that I had to believe they were being honest with me.

"Agent Savoy approached me," Ivy said then, voice dulling out, as though she'd given up all hope but couldn't help herself from expelling the poison knowledge that held her so tightly. "She knew it was me and Dad, but she couldn't prove it. She wanted me to turn on him. *I* wanted out." Ivy shrugged. "She said she'd get me immunity if I gave states evidence. So, I said yes." She stiffened then, rage returning. "Except she backed out of our deal. She lied to me." Ivy's anger receded but the softer, sadder girl didn't return. "Dad was the thief, but I did all the planning. I made sure Savoy had the wrong info, covered our tracks. Served her *right*." She snarled that. "I hope she gets *fired*."

There was an excellent chance she might, if she wasn't a murderer herself. "Ivy," I said, "did your father find out you were working with Savoy?"

When she shook her head, it was with almost violent denial. "He had no idea," she said. "I swear it. And I wasn't going to tell him. I was just going to let him finish this year out then take my cut and leave. Go someplace he'd never track me down. Start over, you know?" She sniffled, shrugged. "I tried to do the right thing. I tried to make a deal." Hope surfaced, to my surprise, the last thing I expected from her as she stared at me for a long moment. "Can I make a deal with *you*?"

That stumped me, but only for a second. "You know where the rest of the stolen items are?"

Ivy nodded instantly. "I can help the police if I get a deal," she said, pulling herself together, sitting up straighter. "But I didn't kill Dad and I won't go down for his murder."

"Ivy." I inhaled, glanced up at Cherise who shook her head. The young woman saw her motion, tensed all over again.

"This is all on Savoy," she snapped at the sheriff. "If she'd just held up her end, this would all be over." Ivy broke down again a moment later, clearly in the grip of a tide of emotions she was finally failing to control as she let out a soft sob. "He made me this way," Ivy whispered. "I could have been so much more."

I was a therapist, for heaven's sake. Trained to help people in terrible positions who thought the worst of themselves and their lives. But at that moment, I couldn't come up with a single comforting word.

What could I possibly say to that?

CHAPTER ELEVEN

I couldn't help but feel for both girls and excused myself for a moment, exiting past Thompson Adams and heading outside for a quick breath of air. Honestly, if Nicholas Bells wasn't already dead... the man should be grateful he wasn't around to face my wrath, let me tell you.

Cherise might not have agreed, but I was leaning toward innocent for both daughters. Either that or Oscars for the two of them, since their Academy Award-level performances—if they were both acting—fooled even my cat.

But I didn't get a say in the matter, not really. This was the sheriff's domain, and I was just a momentary spectator. Then again, she left me to do what I do best, and I knew Cherise valued my opinion, if not my nosiness. I was two deep breaths into deciding to return inside and tell her what I thought regardless of her opinion when Agent Savoy exited her car and marched toward me. So, she hadn't left, then? Spent the last little bit stewing in her SUV? Fair enough. And since she was on my personal suspect list—okay, pretty far down, but she wasn't off the hook in my opinion—I was actually happy to see her.

If only to get the chance to give her a piece of my mind.

"Ms. Pringle," she said before she even hit the stairs.

"Agent," I shot back, cutting her off. "You have a lot to answer for."

That stopped her in her tracks as a flicker of guilt crossed her face. But about what I didn't have a solid answer. I would have been very happy to hear she was the killer, frankly, though that was my personal bias and protectiveness toward the two young women inside showing up. I was well aware of the reasons for my dislike of the tall, lean agent who finally finished her approach and stopped beside me, her few inches in height doing nothing to impress, however.

"I have no idea—" She gave up trying after barely getting started and I can only imagine the look on my face that triggered her abrupt pause.

"You left that poor young woman without options," I snapped. Savoy wavered, nodded. "Why?"

The agent shifted inside her long coat, not meeting my eyes, staring off into the distance. "I made that promise to Ivy intending to keep it." Her voice dropped into sadness and regret. "But my bosses refused to honor it. There was nothing I could do." She shrugged then, as though she'd finally admitted the truth to herself as well as me. "I wish it went differently, Ms. Pringle, but the truth is my hands were tied and I had no choice."

If it were you, would you have stayed mad? I wanted to, trust me. But the defeat in Savoy had me relenting somewhat. "Sheriff King has questions for you," I said, stepping aside and gesturing at the door. "You're not going to like any of them."

Savoy nodded heavily but went inside, not bothering to hold the door for me. Still petty, check. I was feeling rather petty myself, so whatever. But I didn't expect Savoy to march into the bullpen and try to take over again despite her recent admission of guilt. Good thing Cherise seemed more than prepared for such an eventuality, however, because I was abruptly confronted by Thompson Adams who spluttered as he surged to his feet at the sight of the returning agent.

"Arrest her!" Was he talking to me? I bypassed him and carried on. He tried to follow, but Cherise was already raising her arm to point a finger at him.

"Sit!" He did after a minute while she glared down at the agent. "I told you to leave."

"I have information you need," Savoy shot back.

"Like the fact you backed out on a deal with your prime suspect?" Cherise let that sink in, not knowing I'd already dropped that bomb and warned the agent, while Ivy flinched but didn't crumble. The girl's tears had dried up, Holly's hand still in hers. Belladonna had taken over both laps as the girls had pulled their chairs closer together, the front end of my cat in Holly's lap, her huge, fluffy rear and tail in Ivy's.

Savoy didn't even glance at the victim's daughters, shoulders stiff and rigid, entire being wound so tight I worried she might crack. Instead, she raised her chin and spoke.

"My professional conduct is none of your business, Sheriff King," she said in her best FBI voice. I knew it well, heard it more than often enough from my ex-husband. Something about being a federal agent layered in a level of superiority that always made my teeth ache. Probably from clenching my jaw, but there you go.

"Your failure to follow through for a CI *is* my business," Cherise shot back, "especially when that confidential informant is now your favorite suspect." She leaned in as Savoy tried to hold her ground, the agent now pale and wavering, though she did stand, to her credit, despite the heavy tension growing between the two. Foolish, really. She'd already admitted the truth to me. Why not just tell the sheriff as well? Head-butting between branches of law enforcement really was ridiculous.

Cherise was the statuesque epitome of confidence regardless of Savoy's status, and while not a bully was more than capable of intimidating when she needed to. "Tell me, Agent Savoy. Is this so-called information you're now about to share new or something you were holding onto?"

Savoy cleared her throat before she spoke. "This is a federal matter," she said.

"So, something you've been holding back, got it." Cherise let out a heavy exhale but backed down, surprisingly. "Whatever you think you have, there's no proof this is a cross-state case. That means unless you have evidence otherwise, I'm calling in the state police and you can fight it out with them."

"Don't do that." Savoy spoke abruptly before pulling herself back together and leaning in toward Cherise, her turn to try to intimidate. "You don't have to call state. I'm more than willing to share what I have."

"No, you're desperate to prove something," Cherise shot back. "Even if it's the wrong thing. I've seen this before, Savoy. I know that look on your face. You need a win, no matter the cost. But I'm not going to stand by and let you take out your vendetta on these young women. If they are guilty of murder or anything else, that's for a judge and jury to decide."

"Except I have proof the girls were working together," Savoy said. "And that they murdered their father together."

I know you're aware I had this thought myself at one point, but I was no longer willing to entertain it. Cherise, on the other hand, seemed at least open to the conversation while the two girls spluttered and denied it immediately.

"She's lying," Ivy said, arm going around Holly's shoulder.

"You have no proof of anything," Holly said. "There's no proof to find."

"You two," Savoy finally addressed them, "have

been in conversation with one another the last several weeks. I have phone logs," she pulled a paper out of her inside pocket and handed it to Cherise, "that they have been talking since the first of the month."

Okay, was I wrong then? Were they the best actresses the world had ever seen? I couldn't help but stare at Belladonna and wonder if she was losing her touch, too. Except, the sheriff was already frowning as she perused the page, shaking her head.

"Most of these calls lasted seconds," she said. "And originated with one number to the other."

"There's one return," Savoy said, stabbing at the page with her finger. "Just two days ago. It lasted thirty seconds. More than long enough to confirm a murder plot."

Cherise looked up at the girls, both of whom stared back in shock, though Holly immediately started talking as though her attention broke whatever hold the news had over her.

"I got Ivy's number from her mother," she said. "She and my mom stay in touch." Ivy shook her head, whispering something to her sister that looked like *lawyer*, but Holly didn't stop. "I've been calling her, trying to get her to talk to me. She's my sister." More tears, and I hardly blamed her.

Ivy finally tossed her free hand, now holding Holly firmly around her shoulders like she'd never let her go. "I thought she was after a cut of the take," she said, voice growling but clearly an act. "I didn't believe her. Dad said she was just out for money." Ivy turned to Holly then, ignoring the rest of us. "I'm so sorry." She broke down, too, hugging her younger sister. "I should never have listened to him. I wasted so much time."

"It's okay." Now Holly seemed to be the strong one, soothing Ivy and rocking her a little, sweet smile on her face. This is all she wanted in the first place. "We're together now." She met my eyes, hers hardening. "And no one can take that from us."

Holly's disconnect had weakened her. Now that she had Ivy in her life? The turnabout was remarkable. I just hoped it wasn't going to end badly for both of them. They'd already been through enough.

"And the long call?" Cherise spoke up, voice soft and prompting but without anger. She waved off the agent before Savoy could interject with that fury I saw on her face at the explanation. Yup, my friend pegged Savoy correctly.

"I finally got sick of Holly trying to talk to me and called her back," Ivy said. "Told her to leave us alone. I was really mean." Her voice fell, words cracking. "I said some awful things."

"I understand, it's okay." Holly's sweetness wasn't an act and neither was Ivy's hurt. The sisters were telling the truth, I'd stake my life on it.

"It's not okay," Ivy said. "You deserved better." Her chin came up as she faced down Cherise. "Whatever this woman tells you, she's trying to cover her tracks. The truth is, she backed out of our deal and I was forced to do what I always did. If Dad's death is on anyone, it's on you, Agent Savoy."

The FBI agent didn't respond to that accusation,

instead cutting Cherise off as the sheriff tried to speak. "Where are the rest of the heist jewels?" She practically vibrated with intensity, enough that I worried she might lunge at the sisters and use physical force to extract what she wanted. "I already have your fence in custody." Ivy didn't answer, shaking her head. "You have nowhere to sell the haul. Tell me where the other stuff is, and I'll consider our deal."

"It's all fake, remember?" Ivy's nasty smirk wasn't helping her any, though I hardly blamed her.

Savoy's veneer finally cracked as she took a step toward the girls, Cherise forced to grab her and pull her back. I'd seen that level of rage before, but never on the face of someone who had a gun on her hip, and it scared me enough I found myself suddenly standing between the agent and the sisters. Though what my silly brain thought I could do to protect them, I have no idea. I wasn't given a choice.

"Stand down, Agent Savoy," I said.

"Get out of the way," she snarled at me, jerking against Cherise's hand on her arm.

"This is your fault!" Ivy was on her feet, Belladonna leaping up and onto the desk behind the chairs, out of the way and humming her unhappiness. "I just wanted protection from my father. I was going to give you everything you wanted. Was that too much to ask?" Savoy didn't answer as Ivy sat back down. "*You* made this mess."

Of course, I knew better now. Why Savoy didn't decide to own up at that moment, I had no idea. Pride, more than likely, and the anger she still stewed in. Regardless, Ivy was right.

"Sheriff?" We all turned to find the young receptionist standing at the door to the bullpen, a short, round man in a suit and long coat waiting beside her. His mustache bristled as he scowled at the scene unfolding. "The public defender is here."

"I hope you're not interrogating my clients without me present, Sheriff King." I didn't know the man, but Cherise obviously did, nodding to him.

"Harold," she said. "You're representing both sisters?"

He huffed his waddling way past her and Savoy, holding out a card to the girls. "Harold Chester," he said. Before looking me up and down. "And you are?"

"Just trying to help," I said, stepping off and backing away as he motioned for the two girls to stand.

"I'm using your office," Harold said to Cherise over his shoulder as he strode off again, the Bells sisters hesitating before following. I waited until the door closed behind them before exhaling, turning to hold my arms out to Belladonna. She leaped to me and snuggled against me, though her purr didn't return. I spun to put her back in her carrier and exit before I was asked to leave—that was coming, I had no doubt—when I realized someone was missing.

"Where's Thompson Adams?" I turned back toward Cherise who was glaring at Savoy, the pair facing off and ignoring me completely.

Until the FBI agent let out an exasperated breath and fixed me with her judgment. "You are dismissed," she snapped. Any vulnerability she'd shared with me previously had been smothered by her unhealthy drive to dominate this case. Instead, I was faced with the woman she'd become. "Leave. Now."

Of course, I didn't do as I was told. Not by her, at least. I waited for Cherise to fix her attention on me and nod.

"Thanks, Seph," she said. "If I need you, I'll call."

It only took a moment to return Belladonna to the carrier, something she did almost happily, not like her at all. Under normal circumstances, Bella would have been wailing and fighting the confinement. So, even my cat wanted out. Why then did it feel like I was quitting at the worst possible moment when I marched out to my car to do as I was instructed?

CHAPTER TWELVE

I'd just released Belladonna, the cat bounding her way into the living room when I groaned to myself over my distracted mind. Because the moment I looked up, my gaze fell to the display of ornaments Calliope had arranged for me, the gap near the top reminding me that, while I now had a full set, a very expensive piece remained missing at the scene of the crime. And while I stood there and argued with myself about the fact it was just money and I could let it go, seriously, the miserly single woman in me who could use that cash to pamper herself over the holidays?

Refused to let me leave well enough alone.

Honestly, it was a silly thing to worry about. I had the piece I needed. I could picture Callie's happy face. That was more than enough, right?

Right?

Apparently not. "I'll be right back," I called out to Belladonna as I headed out into the chill early afternoon air, the sun already weakening in the sky as the short stint of daylight we had this time of year already mostly over. The last thing I honestly wanted to do was drive across town to the market yet again, but that was exactly what I found myself doing.

Awesome, wasn't it?

Fate had a funny way of twisting me around its fingers, and today was no exception. Because as I grumbled to myself, about as far from the holiday spirit as I could get over not being able to just go home, put my feet up and indulge in a gin or two over the truly horrible day I'd had, I spotted one of the reasons for my present state of mind driving past me with a very unhappy expression on his face. Now, you might choose to judge me for turning around and following Thompson Adams to his destination. Go for it, I won't hold it against you. I really should have left well enough alone, as requested. But I was already thinking along the lines of young women and their predicaments and though Ivy and Holly Bells weren't my responsibility, Calliope's face flashed in my mind, and I knew what she'd say. Or not say, while moping about it. For weeks.

Which had me turning the car around and staying back just far enough my quarry wouldn't notice he was being followed. Not a hard thing to do. Wallace was a small town and so catching up to him was simple enough, the light traffic just sufficient to separate us but not so much I couldn't keep him in my sights.

The question was, where was he going? It did cross my mind he was heading out of town, especially when he turned off the main street and headed toward the interstate ramp. Except, instead of pulling off, he drove under the overpass and steered into the small storage facility that had recently been built just inside town limits. I slowed and stopped, watching him park and hurry inside, avoiding the office, pulling my own car in once he disappeared.

I was just climbing out of my car when a head popped out of the office door, the young man waving at me with a smile.

"Hey, Ms. P," Justin Perrier said. "You need something?"

Wait, he worked here, too? Just my luck. "Justin, awesome." I nodded, gesturing to him as my suspicions about Thompson's presence warranted backup. Yes, I should have called Cherise, but I wanted proof that my leap to conclusion was accurate. But there were very few reasons why someone might rent storage space in a town where their merchandise had recently gone missing, right?

"Mind joining me?" I nodded toward the building's separate entrance to the interior where the individual storage units were housed. "There's someone I need to talk to."

"Is this about the case?" His eyes lit up. "Sure thing." I worried immediately I'd just invited disaster, hesitating over that call to the sheriff after all. But Justin's serious expression and utter lack of excitement felt like he took it seriously enough I carried on. That gravity deepened when I quietly filled him in on where we were going.

"Lead the way, Ms. P," he said, hand on his taser. "I've got your back."

I actually felt better knowing that.

It wasn't hard to find my target, not after Justin dashed inside to check the number of the locker in question. The tall, narrow door stood open, the sound of footsteps inside making me pause as we turned the corner, though the shock on Thompson Adams's face at the sight of me and my companion meant I wasn't far off my guess.

"Mr. Adams," I said with far more authority than I commanded, even with an armed guard at my side. "Time to come clean."

He shifted the black duffle bag in his right hand a little, fighting to control his expression. Failed, though, fear mixing with desperation of his own as he looked back and forth between me and Justin. Who now had his hand on his taser and appeared to know what to do with it even if he wished he had a different weapon at his disposal.

"You have no right," Thompson said.

"Sheriff King is on her way," I lied. "I think she's going to be very interested in what you've got there. Rather than argue with me," I waved off his attempted protest, "why don't you just tell me what actually happened?" I paused a beat. "This will be your only chance to share your side. You know what cops are like."

Oh, I went there, of course, I did. And he fell for it. Sucker.

"None of this was supposed to happen." Panic took over and I watched Thompson waver, was ready for him when he tried to run. But it was Justin who caught him, pinned him down, plastic zip ties binding Thompson's hands while I finally took a second and texted Cherise.

Safe and Secure Storage, I sent. *I found the jewels.*

I didn't bother to check her reply, bending over the bag and unzipping it instead. Revealing, as I'd just told my sheriff friend, the merchandise in question.

Thompson sobbed once, heavily and anguished, as Justin propped him up against the next storage locker, hands cuffed behind him, face so pale I worried he might pass out.

"This isn't what it looks like," Thompson said.

"You stole your own jewels." I waited for him to deny it. Which he couldn't, naturally. Mute now and still in the grip of near hysteria, he simply stared back at me, eyes huge and bulging. "You traded them out for fakes. How did you know Nicholas Bells was going to steal them?"

Thompson groaned, sagging at last. "We had a deal," he said. "He came to me a few years ago. He knew I was having financial trouble and suggested we both get rich."

How had Savoy missed that? Maybe she hadn't but was so fixated on the girls she couldn't see past that focus. Or was this just more information she had been too stubborn to share? I voted for the latter, considering she'd made a fumbled attempt to implicate him in front of Cherise. All this secrecy had only ensured she'd bungle the case.

The fact she'd likely not ever learn the lesson, however? More than a little likely.

"He cheated me," Thompson blurted then. "He wouldn't give me my cut last time. The insurance company barely covered the costs and said if it happened again, I'd only get a partial settlement." Anger replaced his panic briefly. "And Savoy was breathing down my neck." Yes, the thought lingered she might have been part of the problem. He just confirmed she wasn't involved, just keeping things to herself that could have been helpful. Not as bad as being in on it, I guess. Barely. "I had to do something."

"So, you switched the jewels out," I said. It made sense. "Double payday, right? You get to keep the real ones and sell them on the black market while collecting the insurance money you *could* get." Enough to retire on, likely. One score to wrap things up.

"Savoy was going to nail Nicholas at some point," Thompson grunted.

"Revenge, too," I said. "Except, things didn't go the way you planned. Why did you kill him? Did he find out what you'd done?" I thought about the bracelet Holly had in her possession. "He caught you switching the jewels out, so you killed him, is that it?"

"No, I swear!" The broker's panic was back in full force. "I snuck into the tent, yes. I knew where he kept the merchandise, and I switched it after the fact. I'm guilty of all of that. But I didn't kill

Nicholas. He didn't catch me. There was no one there and I got away clean." Thompson let out another sob, this one softer, broken. "I was going to stick it out but then I saw that girl had one of the real pieces. I panicked, I thought I made a mistake."

"You did," I said, standing as I heard the sound of approaching sirens. "And now you're going to pay for it."

Thompson stared up at me, mute once more, while Justin leaned in toward me with a grin.

"And I thought security was boring," he said.

CHAPTER THIRTEEN

I stood beside Cherise with my hands in my pockets, watching as a deputy put Thompson Adams in the back of a squad car. Savoy stood off to one side, on the phone, talking low and fast to someone as she did.

"Nice job," my sheriff friend said. "Don't ever do anything like this again."

I laughed and shrugged, pointing out Justin Perrier to her who stood off to one side, eyes bright and obviously excited by the unfolding drama. "He's a good kid," I said. "I hear he applied to the academy."

Cherise grunted, then sighed with a grin showing up at last. "Yeah, I know," she said. "Seriously, thanks for the help, Seph, but please. Don't take on murderers, okay?"

"At least I wasn't alone this time," I said.

She didn't bother commenting on that, bless her heart.

I waved to Justin on the way out with a flashing grin for him which he returned with a salute. No doubt, he'd be part of the ranks of Wallace's police department before too long, though Cherise was going to have a hard time keeping him, I was sure of that. It wasn't until I pulled out onto the street, heading back toward town, that I realized the reason I was out here in the first place still waited for me to deal with it.

Groan and moan and whatever, Seph.

It took ten minutes to drive to the market. I was relieved to see it was still open, catching the sign at the entrance that told me I had tons of time. Tonight was Santa night, still several hours to go, so getting my property shouldn't be difficult.

Imagine my surprise, as I approached the tent, when I spotted none other than our usual town Santa, Charles Harper in the familiar suit he wore this time of year. I joined him where he stood off to one side of the North Pole plot, shaking his hand.

"I heard you weren't well," I said. "Glad to see you're better, Charles."

He actually blushed under that white beard and mustache of his, winking slowly at me as he glanced sideways before speaking. "Not that sick," he whispered. "Kind of sick and tired." His eye roll had me grinning back. "I'm always Santa," he said. "I just wanted a year off, should have known the gossip mill would blow it out of proportion. But when I heard what happened, well." He laid one finger on the side of his nose and beamed at me. "I couldn't let the kiddies down."

"Fair enough," I said. "But just say no, next time, would you? Some of us worry about you."

He chuckled at that, nodded. "I've already heard it all from Helen," he said. "You'd think I committed murder or something." Charles blanched at that, going serious. "Too soon. Sorry." He hurried away as the lights came on and the lineup of kids started cheering. I stood there in the shadows of the tent, watching him take his ho-ho-hoing seat on the throne, the scurrying form of Helen November orchestrating the eager children's approach, before ducking into the tent.

I searched for a solid ten minutes without avail, the ornament nowhere to be seen. Frustrated, I had to admit defeat and turned toward the flap at the back, not wanting to disturb Santa's show out front. I'd just have to suck up the cost, I guess. Hey, my kid spent over a thousand dollars to buy me those ornaments, so I could swallow a hundred bucks.

Cheapskate.

Except, as I passed a hanging curtain, I realized I'd failed to look everywhere after all. Discarded and unused decorations for the village had been piled in the corner, some clearly broken. I'd kicked the box to keep it from getting stepped on when I'd dropped it. Had it skittered all this way? Or was, perhaps, tossed in the pile with the rest of these discards? Worth the look since I'd come this far.

I can tell you, it wasn't much fun sorting through the remnants of Christmas past. Someone decided this was a garbage heap as much as a place for unneeded decorations to hang out for the duration of the market, so I quickly had dirty hands and a sense of revulsion over the scent of a rotting half-sandwich and several half-empty cups of coffee with the thick cream forming a disgusting skim that ran out when I accidentally bumped them. That mess was paired with the layer of dust on some of the items that clearly hadn't been used in years and had only been transported to this location because no one had taken the time to toss them.

By the time I reached the back of the pile, no ornament to be found, I felt not only defeated but like I needed a thorough shower. I was about to rise and go, write this whole effort off, when I caught sight of something that stopped me in my tracks while wheels turned over in my mind, a truth clicking into place.

I may not have located my property, but I'd just found the murder weapon.

I hung up from calling Cherise to inform her of my find, mind humming, knowing better than to touch the item with my bare hands. But fate came knocking again, leaving me with no choice when someone entered the tent from the far flap and let out a shriek.

My hand reflexively closed around the item as I turned to look. Helen November clutched at her narrow chest with both mittened hands, her fear flashing into nervousness before the bustling busybody took over. She rushed toward me, flapping her hands at me, scowling as the bells on her feet and hat tinkled in counterpoint.

"You're not supposed to be in here," she said.

I held up the decorative candy cane, a match to the ones she'd been fiddling with earlier, this one with a large crease at the top in the shape of someone's head. I could guess whose noggin made that imprint, an easy leap to murder. "And you aren't supposed to kill people. But we can both agree to disagree, I suppose."

She didn't try to deny it, at least, though as she closed the distance between us, I could see Helen November's face held not even a scrap of regret as she stopped in front of me.

"You should have minded your own business." The tiny older woman's tone was threatening enough that I slowly stood, nervous now that I had to face her alone. Where was Cherise? I'd just hung up from telling her what I suspected, so it was going to be a hot minute before she could come to the rescue. I could hear the chatter of the children outside the tent, knew that Santa was still hard at work. Helen had obviously come inside for something, surprising me as much as I surprised her, and would be missed before too long.

Not that I was afraid of the tiny woman, right? Um, yes, actually. Her face twisted into a mask of rage, her eyes burning with some sort of fanatical fury I'd never seen before, not in all my years as a therapist. Madness burned in Helen November and threatened my life as much as I now knew it had taken Nicholas Bells's.

"I know you killed him." I did my best to keep

the murder weapon between us. No, I didn't plan to use it on her or anything, but seriously. I'd never been so creeped out, made worse by the costume she wore, the tinkling of those ridiculous bells. With the sudden feeling I'd somehow fallen into a Hollywood horror movie in which I was the next victim, I stumbled a little over the uneven ground of the tent as I carefully backed away from the clearly vicious woman. "I know you used this to do it." I raised the candy cane just a little. "One of them is missing from around the throne. You hit him with it. But why? The theft? Did you find the jewels and try to rip him off?"

Helen's tiny body vibrated. "You have no idea what you're talking about," she snarled. "Jewels? Who cares about stupid *jewels*." Her disdain cut like a weapon as she stalked me, hovering on the balls of her tinkling shoes, hands stretched out as though she prepared to pounce. The sheer ridiculousness of the situation wasn't lost on me, but it was no laughing matter despite my near-hysterical need to do so. "He was *ruining Christmas*!"

I blinked, floored by that accusation. "What?" I could have tried to be more eloquent, but I was so shocked by her response, I couldn't muster anything else.

She was more than happy to rant, regardless, filling me in on the rest as she raged at me. "That *creature*," she snarled that word through clenched teeth, "was no *Santa*." Okay, crazy lady. And I hated that word, but if the sock fit, yo. "An estranged daughter out of wedlock?" He might as well have kicked a puppy. "Another who he treated like dirt?" Yikes, she was really all-in on her hate for him. "And, to top it all off, he was only doing this for *money*?" That sounded like the worst crime of all in her opinion. Talk about a messed-up sense of honor. "He didn't deserve to wear the suit. He didn't deserve to *live*."

Helen November had gone off her rocker and taken Nicholas Bells out when she fell.

"I had no idea he was a thief." She paced sideways then back again, never taking her eyes from me, hands closing in as though ready to choke the life from me, too. "I heard him complaining about how little they were paying him, that it was time to find another gig." She spit that last word out as though speaking it offended her to her core. Having no idea, I suppose, that it was likely his fence he was talking about, not town council. "Like this was some side hustle he could discard. He was to be Santa. *Santa*." She was so far off into the deep end that I was fairly confident I'd be defending my own life shortly, my hands tightening on the metal candy cane just in case. While hoping someone might intrude, that Cherise might arrive in time. All while struggling to keep my heart from leaping out of me. "It was the last straw, the very end. I confronted him. Told him he wasn't worthy. And he *laughed* at me." Helen shuddered down to her tinkling shoes, eyes bulging while she stopped her pacing and faced me as though I were the man she spoke of. "This is my town, my show. I've been Wallace's elf for forty Christmases, like my father before me. This is a sacred role I play."

Spittle formed in the corners of her mouth while I held my breath and tried not to set her off further. "I've seen Santas come and go. He *fired* me. *Me*." She shivered again, her face finally falling, gaze dropping to her hands held like claws before her. "I couldn't let him near the innocent ones of this town. I couldn't let him ruin Christmas." Her eyes met mine, a flicker of the woman she really was appearing for a moment, sanity the exception now, not the norm. "He said he'd make sure I was done, that I'd seen my last year in this suit." She plucked at her costume like it was the only thing keeping her from flying apart. And it was, obviously. "I didn't mean to kill him." Helen staggered a little, stiffened. "I just…" she gestured at the candy cane in my hands, my own shaking enough the tremble showed, though she didn't seem to notice. "What have I done?"

Cherise picked the perfect time to arrive, just as Helen sank to her knees and sobbed.

CHAPTER FOURTEEN

I sipped my gin, stirring the saucepan of curry as I reviewed the email Cherise had sent.

Helen's being charged with murder, she'd written, *though her lawyer is using the insanity defense, so she may never see the inside of a cell.* I wasn't about to tell my sheriff friend I might have suggested that very thing to the public defender because she didn't need to know. And while Helen November was a murderer, it was very clear to me she'd suffered some kind of psychological break and that she was in need of treatment as much as punishment.

Thompson Adams copped to everything. He's already turned over evidence against the fence he planned to use. He'll be going away for a long time. Good to know. *And I just heard Justin Perrier got accepted to the academy. He's a good kid. I'll see what I can do to help him along.* That had me grinning. I'd already received a thank you call from him earlier and his excitement was palpable.

I know you wish otherwise, but I had to arrest Ivy Bells. Cherise was right about that, and yet I understood completely. While Ivy might have wanted to turn over a new leaf, there was no question she'd spent her life in crime. And though she did so because of her father, she wasn't a minor and her attempt to make a deal with Savoy had solidified her acceptance of her culpability. *But I put in a word with the state's attorney for her just in case it helps.*

It wasn't lost on me that Cherise had as soft a heart as I did sometimes and that had me smiling at the message she'd sent before sending one back.

I spoke to Holly, I wrote as I sipped again, the scent of butter chicken making my kitchen divine. *She and Ivy are making a go of their relationship, so at least Ivy will have support. And their moms are both involved. I think everything will work out, now that their father is out of the picture.*

At least, I hoped so.

Dinner almost done, I topped up my gin from the expensive bottle that arrived at my door that morning. Agent Savoy had hand-delivered it, refusing my invitation to enter and simply shaking my hand.

"Thank you," she said. Paused with a deep breath that ended in a puff of mist in the chilly December air. "I lost sight of myself and the job. Agent Garret said you spoke up for me." I had, made a specific call to my ex for just that reason. I know you're wondering why, but I finally decided the flash of the real agent she was, the woman she showed me on the steps outside the sheriff's office, deserved a chance to pull her life and career back from the brink. The rest would be up to her and if she sank, so be it.

Call it Christmas compassion or whatever you want, but I had been feeling charitable, okay? It had taken some convincing, and Trent telling me to stay out of it, but I'd finally gotten my message across. I didn't owe her anything, but I understood the pressures of her position. "The Bureau mandated therapy." She wrinkled her nose at me before sighing again. "But I get to keep my job."

"If I can do anything," I said and meant it.

"You already have." Savoy had waved and left, leaving me with the gift bag that, it turned out, held the pricey bottle I now savored the contents of.

I glanced up into the living room, the overhead lights unlit but the Christmas string Calliope had hung around the picture window glowing in the darkness. The white bulbs reflected from the twelve ornaments hanging there. Wherever the mismarked ten lords had ended up, I was now out of luck, my attempt to find the missing piece gone, the market over. It seemed like a truly minor inconvenience at this point. I was anticipating instead my daughter's excitement to see the one she thought she'd bought hung in my window.

Worth a hundred bucks, hands down.

Speaking of whom. As I leaned against the counter and debated if I was even hungry now, I realized that this whole first year thing was getting a little old, at least in certain circumstances. My need for independence came from my longing for freedom, but as I accepted that it wasn't aloneness I'd wanted, necessarily, just the ability to make my own choices without being attached to someone who didn't love me the way I needed, I realized giving all the leeway to Trent for Thanksgiving, Christmas, every holiday, was just a reflex. Guilt over stepping away from our marriage had undercut my truth.

Because the truth was, I wanted my kid for Christmas, darn it.

Was she somehow listening in to my thoughts or something? Of course not, though it certainly seemed like it. Just as the understanding landed and I fought off stinging tears and a thickening throat at my awareness, the front door opened, and Calliope and Thalia hustled through. Their laughter and chatter, voices calling out for me, quickly quashed my emotional moment and I hurried to hug them both, the cold that clung to them making me shiver.

"Mom," Callie gushed in her usual enthusiasm while Thalia smiled shyly back, "I have the best news." She tossed her coat aside and helped herself to my house, just the way I liked it. "Dad decided to go to Colorado to see Aunt Kimmie for Christmas." She spun around and spread her arms wide with a giant grin.

"You're going to Colorado?" Okay, now I really *was* going to break down.

"No, silly." She hugged me again. "We're going to spend it with you." And then, just like that, she started to cry herself.

Thalia crossed to us, joining our hug, as the three

of us stared through tears at the complete set of ornaments hanging in the window.

"Merry Christmas, Seph," Thalia said.

"Merry Christmas, Mom," Calliope said.

"Merry Christmas," I managed to whisper.

The best Christmas *ever*.

ABOUT THE AUTHOR

Everything you need to know about me is in this one statement: I've wanted to be a writer since I was a little girl, and now I'm doing it. How cool is that, being able to follow your dream and make it reality? I've tried everything from university to college, graduating the second with a journalism diploma (I sucked at telling real stories), and am an enthusiastic improv performer (if you've never tried it, I highly recommend making things up as you go along as often as possible). I've even been in a Celtic girl band (some of our stuff is on YouTube!) and was an independent filmmaker (go check out the Lovely Witches Club). My life has been one creative thing after another—all leading me here, to writing books for a living.

Now with multiple series in happy publication, I live on beautiful and magical Prince Edward Island (I know you've heard of Anne of Green Gables) with my multitude of pets.

I love-love-love hearing from you! You can reach me (and I promise I'll message back) at https://patti@pattilarsen.com. And if you're eager for your next dose of Patti Larsen books (usually about one release a month) come join my mailing list! All the best up and coming, giveaways, contests and, of course, my observations on the world (aren't you just dying to know what I think about everything?) all in one place: https://bit.ly/PattiLarsenEmail.

Last—but not least!—I hope you enjoyed what you read! Your happiness is my happiness. And I'd love to hear just what you thought. A review where you found this book would mean the world to me—reviews feed writers more than you will ever know. So, loved it (or not so much), your honest review would make my day. Thank you!